About

Arianne Richmonde is the *USA TODAY* bestselling author of suspense novel, *Stolen Grace* and the Pearl Series contemporary romance – *Shades of Pearl, Shadows of Pearl, Shimmers of Pearl, Pearl,* and *Belle Pearl.* Arianne is an American author who was raised in both the US and Europe and now lives in France with her husband and coterie of animals. She used to be an actress, and the *Beautiful Chaos Series* is inspired by her past career—she is a huge fan of TV, film, and theatre and loves nothing better than a great performance.

Acknowledgements

Thank you, my Pearlettes and my wonderful team—you know who you are.

Falling Star

(A Beautiful Chaos book)

by
ARIANNE
RICHMONDE

This is the second book in the
Beautiful Chaos Trilogy:

Shooting Star

Falling Star

Shining Star

FEB 2017

In all chaos there is a cosmos, in all disorder a secret order.

Carl Jung

U H-OH, I WAS IN SERIOUS TROUBLE. I hadn't meant it to go that far, but I couldn't stop myself. Jake was hotter—way hotter—than any guy I'd fooled around with. The orgasm he gave me ripped my world apart. My first, ever, with a guy. Left me shattered, confused, wanting more. It was the biggest—most unexpected—surprise of my life. No man had even come close to doing that to me—ever. I mean, they'd tried but failed miserably. Before, I'd always been able to lie back and "count sheep." It was a power thing, I guess. Knowing I had control—never really letting go, mainly because I just didn't feel that there was anything special going on.

But my experience with Jake felt surreal. It was almost as if I, Star Davis, was not even there, but some inner force that had taken over. The temptation to give myself to him was overpowering, but I knew what would happen: he'd fuck me and then never want to have anything to do with me again. Conquest over. At the last second, *almost* before it was too late, I snapped out of *The Twilight Zone* and into the real world.

"Party's over, Jake," I told him, pushing him away. My voice was shaky. The words came out of my mouth, although my alter ego was horrified that I was spoiling all the fun. But I said emphatically, so there was no misinterpretation: "I'm serious—this is as far as I go."

Lying on his sofa like that; open to him and vulnerable, had made me lose my sense of self. I'd let emotion overcome me and knew that if I wanted to keep control and stay professional I needed to get a grip. This role of Skye in *Skye's The Limit* was my second chance—maybe my last chance—and I couldn't screw things up. I needed to come clean with the truth. The Virgin truth. And when I told him I watched his face as it smashed—figuratively speaking—to the floor. He was so shocked, I almost felt sorry for him. But then I quickly remembered that he was a *man*.

Men. Ninety-nine percent of them? Assholes. Unless, of course, you have them under control. Begging. Salivating for more.

Then they can be pussycats.

Go ahead, call me unjust. Or a bitch. But this handy information was drummed into me by my mom ever since I could talk. Or at least, listen. My father? He's not my biological father. He's the man who came and picked my mom up off the ground when she was pregnant with me. HE—the bastard who impregnated her—the one with whom she had fallen head over heels in love—simply took off "to chase another piece of skirt" as Mom so often told me when she was in one of her "talkative" moods. So, as much as my dad pissed me off, I owed him one. He tried. He'd raised me as best he could and it wasn't his fault that Mom was never seriously in love with him.

Anyway, although I felt powerful for a second with Jake, and triumphant, it wasn't long before he crushed me with his nonchalant "Who-gives-a-shit-little-girl-I-won't-waste-my-time-on-you-anyway" kind of attitude. I lay there, yearning for him to hug me, to profess his undying something-or-other for me. But he just laughed cockily like I was nothing to him. An inconvenience.

I guess I was. Nothing, I mean. He could get anyone. And he had. The list was long, longer than the long-limbed movie stars and models he'd "dated" one after another.

"Get dressed. We're going out," Jake announced, as I still lay on the sofa, naked.

"Oh, okay, cool." I felt renewed hope. He was going to take me to some romantic, candlelit dinner and woo me in other ways. Slowly. Take his time.

I got up from the couch and made my way to the bedroom, wondering what I should wear. Something elegant. Sexy. Something more mature, that showed I was a lady not just a teenager. I had some diamond drop earrings I could wear and a sexy Stella McCartney black jersey dress that hugged my curves. But as I was making my way up the stairs my romantic musings were instantly crushed. Jake was on the phone:

"Great, Leo, see you there—yeah, bring the whole crowd if you like. The more the merrier."

And that was how things carried on after our "episode" on the sofa. Jake made darn sure that we were never alone. Friends, producers, friends of friends. And actresses. Everywhere. Eyeing him up, grinning at him inanely like whole rooms full of Cheshire Cats, straight out of *Alice In Wonderland*. We were constantly surrounded, but at the same time, he never took his eyes off me—not because he was crazy about me, I realized—but to make sure I wouldn't escape and go off and swig vodka or something.

And then, in the week that followed, I thought he'd go back to ignoring me but it was worse.

Far worse.

He was sweet and tender. Like an older brother. Putting his arm around me but in a very non-sexual way. Listening to my every word with attention. Once we started filming he'd do a re-take if I wasn't happy with the shot. All over me, but in a "Thoughtful Director" kind of way. It was sickening. It made me hate him. Obsess about him. It wasn't *him* salivating, it was me. Inside. And when I say "inside" that's what I mean. South of my waist, I was a hot mess. Every time he touched me, I wanted to scream with frustration. Remembering the gift he gave me of discovering my sexuality, yet treating it as if it were nothing. I was in turmoil. I was just another girl to him—someone he could do happily without. Yet his kindness was killing me. "Killing me softly."

Little did Jake know I didn't need any liquor to get high. Because I was high in another way, and it was worse than any drug. Constantly craving more . . .

Of him.

"Star, would you like another soda? A coffee? A snack?" It was Biff, Jake's assistant, asking me for the umpteenth time if I needed anything. She had become my right hand man. Yes "man", with her deep voice and lesbian attention. At first I was horrified, told Jake I didn't want her anywhere near me (after what happened to me when I was a girl), but Biff turned out to be the sweetest, gentlest character, so I let her spoil me. The irony was; it wasn't Jake Wild who had fallen for me, it was Biff.

"I'm fine thanks, Biff." We were on set, me in make-up and jail costume, waiting for my scene. There was a hair in the gate and the cameraman wanted to go again. A shame because the take had been pure perfection.

"And . . . action!" Jake barked. The set suddenly became bathed in an eerie silence as Meryl stared into space, then rolled her eyes just a touch to the side. To anyone normal it looked like she was doing nothing, but we in the business knew better. This was another Oscar-worthy performance, fused with subtlety and genius. I never tired of observing her and didn't care about waiting forever to do my scene. The movie set had been my drama school all these years and never more than now. Some of the other actors were in their trailers, doing crosswords or surfing on their laptops. But I stayed rooted to the set because I wanted to watch Jake and Meryl work.

I watched him get close to her and mutter in her ear. Even though she was a consummate star and Jake so young, he didn't feel intimidated by her. I saw her nod and then laugh as if what he'd said was a fantastic idea. Leo was running around, checking things were in order, and Make-up and Hair swooped in on Meryl with combs and face powder. Letting her nose and forehead be dusted to get rid of any shine, she tucked her knees under her, closed her eyes and took a deep breath. Preparing for the next take: the one where you really see how nuts her character is.

Biff drew up a director's chair and sidled next to me. "What do you think of Meryl?" she whispered.

"I think she's the best actor I've ever seen," I said. "She's Bobby de Niro's all-time favorite actress, did you know that?"

"That's praise coming from *him*."

"Sure is."

"I'd like to stay but I have to go and collect Jake's girlfriend from the airport."

I felt my stomach fall a thousand feet. I looked up from my mug of coffee at Biff. Surely she'd made a mistake? "*Girlfriend?*" I hissed, "Jake doesn't have 'girlfriends.' "

"I know, right? But he keeps referring to this one as his 'girlfriend', News to me, but hey, I'm his assistant, I can't ask too many personal questions—it's none of my business."

I felt waves of florescent green wash through me. Jealousy wasn't an emotion I was used to. "Well it *is* your business actually, Biff," I said, in a crazed effort to make sense of all this. "You have to be ahead of him in every way. Understand his needs, his whims, his weaknesses. That is, if you want to be the perfect assistant," I added manipulatively. I knew I'd be able to wheedle info out of Biff at a moment's notice, and this 'girlfriend' topic would be high on my list of priorities.

Biff's eyes were puppy dog eyes. Eager to please, innocent. "I do want to be a great assistant, I do. I love my job so much—I want him to be pleased with my work."

"An assistant has to be like a second brain, a second heart. You have to know *everything* about Jake to be his right arm."

Biff gazed at me lovingly. "I wish *you* were his girlfriend," she said. "Then we'd still see each other even after the movie is over."

"Me? I wouldn't date Jake Wild if he were the last man alive." The words tumbled out of my mouth—I couldn't stop them. I laughed—too falsely. Too loud—Meryl looked up at me from across the set. She smiled distractedly and slipped back to her thoughts. I felt tears well in my eyes and my throat tighten.

Biff touched my hand. "Are you okay, Star? Can I get you anything?"

"I'm just preparing my next scene," I lied. "So who is this 'girlfriend?' "

"Her name's Cassie . . . Cassandra."

"She'll bring him bad luck," I quipped.

"Why?"

I toyed with my prison-knotty hair—they'd backcombed it for my next scene as I was meant to look rough. "Don't you know about the Greek legend? Cassandra had the gift of prophecy but was never believed. She could see into the future but everyone thought she was crazy."

"I've Skyped with her," Biff said. "She's not his usual type."

"Oh yeah? What does she look like?" and then

more urgently, "where did he meet her?"

"Quiet on set please, we're going for another take!" shouted Leo. There was the loud snap of the clapperboard. "Take six. And lights! Camera? Silence please, camera's rolling!"

"And action!" Jake said.

I couldn't concentrate. My pulse was pounding so loudly I thought it would mess up the take— that the sound engineers would be able to hear the 'boom boom' of my heart hammering through my chest with their sensitive headphones that picked up the tiniest of noises. Meryl was prodding her arm with a sharp object, her mouth twisted with disgust at herself.

"And . . . cut! Perfect, Meryl. Have we got that in the can?"

"Just checking the gate," Leo said.

I grabbed Biff by the wrist. "Where did he meet her, Biff?"

"She's an ex. Well, kind of."

"An ex? Is she pretty?"

"Okay, I guess. Nothing special. Nothing like you, Star."

"So how did they hook up again?" I tried to

sound vague, like I was making casual conversation. Not.

"I'm not sure . . . it's like something from a long time ago. You know, a teenage thing rekindled."

"Rekindled?" I stared at Jake who was smiling with happiness and punching the air with his fist. "Can't wait to see the dailies—that was perfect," he was saying to Leo. Jake turned to me, catching my eye, his crooked smile piercing me—our sweet short-lived moment an ever-present memory, haunting me by the second. But my gaze in return was spiked with shards of glass. I forced a grin back. He was wearing fatigues, loose on his hips, his hard stomach peeking through. His dark blond hair disheveled, a dusting of five o'clock shadow on his jaw which made him look sexily tired—a man who'd worked a little too hard but his passion giving him an air of personal triumph. *Passion?* The thought of that word felt thick in my brain . . . passion for *what?* For Cassandra? Ugh! Yet what right did I have over him? He wasn't my boyfriend and he'd made me no promises. The opposite— he'd warned me against himself, telling me he was "bad" and that I should keep away from him.

He sauntered toward me, still grinning. I felt an unbidden tear tumble down my cheek. He scrunched his brow. "Star, what's wrong?" A fatherly 'what's wrong.'

You've got a girlfriend, that's what's goddamn wrong! "Nothing. You know, just feel emotional after Meryl's scene."

"Yeah, she's the best. Looking forward to yours, next." He snuck a glance at his watch. "You ready? We should be alright to roll in ten minutes or so."

I looked up at him. "I thought I'd play it down, you know? Low-key. So you can come in close."

"Well I had planned to start with a two-shot."

"If you could do the close-up first you'd be doing me a favor. If Meryl doesn't mind? I'm feeling the scene right now, you know? If we could go soon, that would be great."

"Sure, Star." He stood tall and yelled, "I want the next shot ready in five! Leo, get this close-up going—yeah, close-up, not a two-shot—tell Paul, like, now! Make-up? Hair? Are we ready?"

My make-up artist, Miriam, came flying over, and so began the fussing. She had maroon-colored powder on the tip of a brush. I was meant to look baggy-eyed and hollow which was a good thing, because I suddenly—after the humdinger girlfriend news—felt like death warmed over.

Ten minutes later, after Jake called "action" I motionlessly started the scene. I let the tears build slowly, well up, and overflow in streams down my face without wiping them away. I stared at Meryl, imagining her to be the ex, Cassandra, the one taking my light away. I imagined my brother and the damage he'd done. I looked up and stared at the ceiling. I could hear the cameras rolling and silence dance around my ears. I glanced at Meryl. Her lips twisted in spiteful anguish—her character taking her over on command as she let a flicker of a mean smile play on her lips. But the camera was on me, not her; a close-up—just my face and neck, so any expression I made would be giant on screen. Meryl was just being generous—as always—helping my character, Skye, feel pain. In an instant, I let rip. A roar escaped me, like a wild animal caught in a trap. I had meant my performance to be nuanced and small but my instinct took over. I felt immersed in loneliness. A single star in the sky. Alone. I gripped my hair, using my hands like talons and started pulling so my scalp felt raw. Was I overacting? Maybe, but I felt it inside—I really did. I finally said my lines, gritted between my teeth. "You . . . you are . . . an evil. . . . *bitch*." Silence rolled on for twenty seconds. I held my gaze, pinning my eyes on Meryl's. She continued to smirk—her character a cruel force of bastardized nature.

"Cut!" Jake said quietly. But the camera kept rolling. This is sometimes what happens when a crew becomes invested in a scene. I carried on acting, despite Jake having said 'cut' . . . I could hear that wonderful, calming whirr of the camera . . . a sound that was like my second breath . . . my life . . . my existence . . .

"That's a wrap for now," and then louder, "Cut!" I let my eyes wander to Jake's face. And then he mouthed to me silently, "I love you."

My stomach flipped. Seriously? Did I read him right? But then he added out loud, "I love you, Star, I love you, Meryl! I love *all* of you for the best day's filming ever!"

And I fell back down to earth again. Wondering if I'd ever hear those words for real.

PRODUCTION Falling Star

DIRECTOR Jake Wild   DATE June

SCENE Leo and Jake   TAKE 2

CAMERA Jake Wild

"TAKE FIVE, EVERYONE, we all need a quick break. Actually, let's say fifteen minutes."

Leo grinned at me. "Good day, my friend, good day."

"You did great, Leo. Love those sharp shadows you set up for Paul. Meryl looked fucking crazy. And Star—well, what can I say?"

"She's great actress—perfect casting, Jake. That last scene? you could not hear pin drop. Wanna grab beer?"

I smiled. I loved Leo's Russian accent and how

he got expressions muddled up. "Sure, let's go to my trailer." I yelled out so everyone could hear, "Back in ten, everyone."

Leo and I made our way through the lot and, once in my trailer, I slumped onto the couch, while Leo took some ice-cold beers from the fridge and grabbed some snacks from the kitchenette. He threw the packets on the table where I had my feet parked. I was dog-tired but at the same time high on excitement and energy. Star was showing me what she was made of. Fuck, that girl could act. She was resilient but vulnerable at the same time. She turned me on in every way—mentally, physically, emotionally—but the Reason chip inside my head kept spelling it out loud and clear, *No, Jake. Leave her alone. She's a young girl. Too young. A goddamn virgin, on top of it all.*

Leave. Her. Alone.

"Looking forward to Badlands?" Leo asked, ripping open a bag of potato chips.

"Yeah, a lot. Except—"

"What?" he sat down and handed me a beer.

"Things are going to be a bit different. You know, with Cassie on board."

"So who is Cassie chick you told me about?

She cute?"

"Not really. I mean, yeah, pretty, but not the type to turn heads."

"Fuck, man? I thought you went for babes?"

"I told you, Leo, I'm done with babes. I'm *done* fucking around. But at the same time I've been going crazy being abstinent. I've decided I need a *real* girlfriend. Someone stable. Intelligent. Someone I can trust with my life."

"Your life? You flying to Mars or something?"

"Just a nice, friendly, clever woman to keep me sane. No drama, no crazy games, no drugs or parties. Just a sweet, uncomplicated, easygoing girl. We've known each other forever. We're old mates. She's always been there for me. Crazy about me."

"Cool, so Star's game? . . . I mean, free?"

I froze. The idea of anyone, least of all Leo, touching Star, caused a rush of adrenaline to kick into my system as if I were running from a bear or lion. "Very funny, Leo. Leave my cast members alone."

"Anyway, not sure what Cassie thing is all about. You like *Star*," Leo said, nodding his head like he knew it all. "Star's girl for you."

"Off limits, Leo," I said, realizing that I'd

obviously made my feelings for Star apparent. "I told you. It ain't gonna happen! That's why I sent for Cassie—should be arriving any minute now. I gave her a job as Continuity so she'd have something to do. I want to see if I can make a real relationship work. A real girlfriend/boyfriend thing."

"And then what?"

"What do you mean?"

"When you get bored of Ms. Goody-Two-Shoes? After five long minutes?"

"She's very clever. Went to Oxford, has a degree in Classics. She's smart, I won't get bored—she's a great conversationalist."

Leo burst out laughing. "Yeah, pussies can really talk."

"There's more to life than great pussy, Leo. Look, we'd better get back to the set. I want a muted, very arty look for the next scene, in keeping with that last angular shot of Meryl. Love what you did by the way, Leo—the ideas you gave Paul. I thought he was the best DP I'd ever had but man, you're doing great stuff. Keep this up and you'll be working for me for as long as you want."

8. is Star

BACK IN MY TRAILER, I waited for Dr. Deal—Narissa, as she preferred to be addressed. The paparazzi were trailing me everywhere, ever since they'd gotten wind of the fact I was living at Jake's house. "Hollywood's most beautiful young couple," they said. "THE NEW BRANGELINA?" another headline said— "WATCH THIS SPACE."

Well I *was* watching this space and getting tired of seeing blank.

It all started after the "episode," when Jake made sure that we were never alone together. Restaurants or friends' houses, or he invited them over to his place—anywhere but in an intimate situation. He had encouraged me to invite my own friends too; Janice and Mindy—anyone who wanted to tag along. We were quite an entourage. Leo, and half the crew, hanging out—Jake and I always had company. Still, the press now knew where to find me because I was no longer hidden away. If we went out we'd always get back to Jake's house before midnight—we were hardly burning the candle at both ends, and no drinking. But it was tiring even for me: the consummate party girl. Tiring mainly because I was no longer doing drugs or drinking, so I was aware of time passing as if in slow motion. Being with him but not able to touch him. Knowing that the precious moment we'd shared had been a one-off, a blip as far as he was concerned, never to be repeated.

At the end of each evening, Biff would escort me to my bedroom and literally, like some strict chaperone, turn out the light. I yearned to stay home alone with Jake, the way we had before the "event" –no such luck. Some nights I was tempted to run away, just to force him to come looking for me—to *react*, show me he cared, but the house alarms were on so if I snuck out of a window, I'd get caught. Besides, sometimes I'd hear his car start up—he was going somewhere after "lights out" but would never tell me where.

My shrink gingerly tapped on my trailer door, jolting me out of my Jake thoughts. "Come in," I called out. She entered, carefully climbing the steps, her smooth silver-gray bob, piecing blue eyes, and pencil skirt suit gave her an air of Vogue model sleekness. Well, an over 50's Vogue model.

"You could fit a family of six in here," Dr. Deal remarked.

"Yeah, well, the trailer which I was raised in was less than half this size. Thanks so much for coming—it's getting kind of crazy with the press—they'd follow me to your office, for sure. I really don't need the 'STAR DAVIS SEES SHRINK' headlines right now. Come sit down. Something to drink? Tea, coffee, juice?"

"Some water would be lovely."

"Still, sparkling? Flavored?" I headed to the kitchen area.

"You're being treated like royalty I see," she said, looking around, "any old water is just fine."

I poured her a Perrier. "Ice, lemon?"

"No thanks."

"We're going on location tomorrow—to South Dakota to the Badlands—so this will be my little sanctuary for a while."

"Is that why this trailer's so big, because there are two of you?"

"Two?"

Narissa nodded.

"Oh, I get it," I said, "you've been listening to the news, huh?"

"I had no choice. I like to keep up to date with my clients. You cancelled our last three sessions so I figured there must be a reason. Too involved to see me—that was my guess."

"Work, that's all. No boyfriend. Don't believe what you read." I sat down and handed Narissa her water. "Look, Narissa, this whole 'Star Davis goes through men like Kleenex' is so not true. I mean, okay, I've had a string of boyfriends but really nothing serious. Sexually speaking, anyway."

"I'm not here to judge you, Star."

"I'm a virgin," I blurted out, "and that's a fact. It's something I keep to myself."

Her pale blue eyes regarded me with fascination as if I were some rare, on-the bridge-of-extinction species.

"I'm not kidding," I added.

She leaned in—her elbows planted on the table, and looked me hard in the eye. "Then why? *Why* are you letting the world believe otherwise? You're still only nineteen. Being a virgin is something to be proud of, not deny."

I shrugged. "I really don't want to be the poster child for Virginity with a capital V."

"But you're happy to be the poster child for . . . for . . . " she didn't finish her sentence.

"Remember Brooke Shields?" I asked. "Her superstardom was before I was born, but we did a job together a few years ago—she played my mom. Lovely person. I checked out her old commercials on YouTube—you know, I always like to see the work of my co-stars before we start shooting. 1981, she was lying on the floor seductively, her jeans tight as hell and said—straight to the camera—'You wanna know what comes between me and my Calvins? Nothing.'

Narissa looked blank.

I clarified, "The commercial she did for Calvin Klein Jeans when she was still a teenager? Playing on the whole virtue, virgin thing? And at the same time being an international sex symbol?"

Narissa nodded—a confused expression etched on her face.

"I don't want a whole big deal made, you know? It's kind of perverse, people speculating on your virginity when you're in the public eye. It's my private life! Virginity doesn't sound so rock 'n roll, either. I mean, come on, my last job I played a stripper—if they'd thought I was all innocent I would never have gotten the part. You can't give them too much information or it goes against you. Why do gay actors pretend they're straight, for instance? Because if people know they're gay they won't get to play the heartthrob. Rock Hudson, Montgomery Clift?—you think they would have been kissing Liz Taylor if everyone had known they were homosexual? And there are plenty of modern-day, gay movie stars—just that the general public have no idea who they are, and these actors go to great lengths to keep it that way. Same principle goes for me. I don't want to lose cool parts based on people's preconceptions of me. Let them think what they like—I know who I am."

Narissa locked her eyes with mine. "Do you, Star? Do you really?"

There was a loud tapping at the door. Saved by the bell. Her last question threw me. Did I know who I was? Actually, if I were to be honest with myself, no, I didn't.

"Yes?" I called out. My trailer door opened and a face peered in: a woman, somewhere between the age of twenty-five and thirty. She had short brown hair, in a sort of pixie cut. Thin. Skinny actually. Converse hightops. Torn jeans. Attractive, but no big deal. I wondered what she was doing here—I'd never seen her before.

"Oh, I'm sorry. I'm looking for Jason. So this isn't *his* Winnebago?" Her accent was very British. Winny Baaygo. She dragged the syllables. Vey "posh" . . . *Downton Abbey* style.

"Jason? I don't know a Jason and I'm pretty familiar with all the crew's names. This is the lot for *Skye's The Limit*. Are you lost or something?"

She was fiddling with the door handle. "Oh, right, I forgot. You all call him Jake. Sorry, I should have introduced myself. You must be Star. I'm Cassie. Jason's—I mean Jake's . . . um, well . . . other half, so to speak."

A wave of nausea washed through me. "Other half of what?" I heard myself say. Cassandra laughed edgily. I didn't invite her inside. "Nice to meet you," I said in a sugary tone but not extending my hand. "I'd invite you in, but I'm in the middle of a meeting."

"Oh, yah, I'm sorry, how rude of me."

Yah, what the hell kind of talk was 'yah'?

"Well, I'm working on this film too," she said, "so we'll see a lot of each other, I suppose."

I swallowed hard—my throat felt like wood. *How much worse could things get?* "What's your job?" I asked, trying not to sound as if I wanted to punch her in the face.

"Oh, I'm the continuity girl. Filling in for Susan while we're in the Badlands."

I wanted to say, *calamity*, not continuity.

She giggled and put her hand over her mouth as if she'd made a *faux pas*. "Hah! that's not very P.C., is it? In America, I mean. Nobody says 'girl' anymore, nor 'actress.' I'm Continuity."

Cassandra—her cheeks flushed with embarrassment—looked at Narissa for support. "Bye," she said awkwardly, giving a little wave, and then she skipped off the steps. Bouncy. Jolly. Annoyingly "perky." I hated her already. Continuity? I wanted her to *continue* right back to England, and never come back.

Jake was really named *Jason*? It didn't suit him one bit. Made me aware of how little I really knew him. I gave her a feeble smile, trying not to be a bitch. It wasn't her fault that she was in my way. Or was it? When had Jake summoned her into his life? Just recently, as Biff seemed to think? Or had Cassandra—Cassie—been around the whole time? When he had me splayed on his couch, his head between my legs, was she *already* his girlfriend *then*? I wondered exactly how and *when* she'd materialized on the scene. *My* scene. Where she abso-fucking-lutely did *not* belong.

"P.C?" I mumbled.

"Politically correct," Narissa said. "I take it she's the competition?"

"Competition?"

"Yes, the girlfriend of the man you like."

"Do you mind, Narissa? I think I'm done with our session for now, I'm not feeling so hot. Was up at five, you know. Trials of the job. Can we take a rain check?"

"You'll have to face the music sooner or later, Star, and I don't think this is a good policy of yours, habitually ending our sessions before the allotted time is up."

"Oh."

"I think we need to talk about your relationship with Jake Wild."

I wanted to roll my eyes but stopped myself. This shrink was relentless. "We don't have a relationship, as such."

"You're living in his home, that's a relationship, with or without sex."

"Tonight's the last night. I'll be here in this trailer on location from tomorrow, and then moving back to my own house after we're done filming there. He's my director, that's all." I could feel my eyes moisten so I turned my head and, wiping away a tear, pretended I was smoothing back a lock of my hair.

"Then why do I sense such vulnerability when

you mention his name?"

"I'm fine."

"What do you want from the relationship? From him?"

I shook my head. "I don't know. I guess I want him to—" I broke off. *I want him to love me.*

"Is this about control, Star? Or about genuine, heartfelt feelings?"

"I don't know," I said, and it was true. I wasn't sure. I had always played with men and I couldn't know if I felt crazy about Jake because he wasn't falling for me, or if I *really* wanted him. All I knew was that the possibility of Jake loving another woman was making me feel sick to my stomach. And that every time he walked into a room, my heart rejoiced, and when he smiled at me my body tingled all over, and when he touched me I practically fell apart.

"Well," Narissa concluded, looking at her watch, "I guess whatever your feelings are, you'll have to put them aside because he has a girlfriend."

I could feel a surge of fury spike my veins. "Then why are we discussing this?" I snapped.

"Why are you trying to wheedle emotions out of me if it's a lost cause anyway? Do you get a kick out of that?"

Narissa remained impassive—her icy eyes giving nothing away. "Of course not, Star. I just want you to be aware of your feelings and your motivations, that's all. And once you understand the root of them, it will help you move on. We'll speak about all this when you're back from location. Good luck with filming and don't do anything bad in the Badlands."

I didn't smile at her lame joke. I just said, "Don't say good luck."

"Why ever not?"

"Because in my business—in the theatre at least—wishing people good luck is bad luck. You tell them to 'break a leg.' Once someone wished me good luck and I fell down some stairs."

"Well break a leg then, Star."

"Thank you, I will."

PRODUCTION
Falling Star

DIRECTOR
Jake Wild

DATE
June

SCENE
Get rid of her

TAKE
4

CAMERA
Jake Wild

"WHAT THE HELL do you think you're doing?"

"Well hello to you, too, Star."

"Are you alone?"

I looked at my watch. "I've got ten minutes. What can I do for you, Star?"

"Why are you playing games with me?" There was defiance in her eyes but they also shimmered as if she might burst out crying any second.

"Calm down, Star, I don't even know what you're talking about."

"Get rid of her."

"Who?"

"You know damn well who! Your *girlfriend*!"

I looked down at my storyboard and realized there was an important shot missing from the next scene—Star being around so much was making me lose concentration "My girlfriend is no concern of yours."

"Yes, she is! I can't work. I can't concentrate!"

I laughed. "She's been here all of two hours and you haven't even started your next scene yet. In fact, unless I'm mistaken, your next scene is in the Badlands and you're done for the day so why don't you go home, take a shower and I'll see you later."

"Are you nuts? You think I'm going back to your house to listen to the bedsprings squeak while you're fucking that . . . that . . . English—"

"Her name's Cassie."

"You're a real heartless bastard, you know that?" she yelled, and then quietly muttered, "I hate you, Jake Wild." She stood on the steps, at the doorway of my trailer, still not stepping inside, but not leaving either.

"No you don't hate me. Come here, Star, let's talk this over." She was glowering at me, still in her prison uniform—her hair a ratty, tangled mess. Make up had made her look sallow and bruised but even so, she was still as beautiful as ever.

"Where is she?" Star demanded.

"In a meeting with the producers."

"Here, on the lot?"

"No, she drove herself to Century City."

"I thought Biff was chauffeuring her around?"

"No, Cassie's using my car."

"She's *driving* your Tesla S? Your beautiful new electric *car*?"

"I'm lending it to her."

"Ugh!"

"Step inside, Star, and close the door. I really don't think we need anyone else to be party to any dramatic scene, off-set."

Star slammed the door and stood there, speechless. What could she say? She wasn't my girlfriend and had made it clear to me that if I wanted more than a kiss I'd need to practically ask for her hand in marriage. She was a nineteen-year-old who had a crush on me, nothing more, and this whole non-affair needed to be nipped in the bud. Now. Before it got out of control.

"I think you're being very unprofessional using

someone for Continuity who isn't trained. It's not an easy job and you're compromising the quality of this movie by hiring her."

"Star, Cassie has worked for the BBC and on film sets before. She's not a complete novice."

"Why is she calling herself a Continuity Girl, then? Has she no self-respect? Her job title is 'Script Supervisor.' I don't like this air of unprofessionalism. I want to know I can rely on the crew, and that they're not off fucking my director somewhere."

Her jealousy was giving me a hard-on. I could smell her; sweet, like jasmine or roses—her eyes fiery; the blue in her irises, greener than usual. Was it true? Did people go green with envy? My lips twitched into a full-on smile. "*My* director?"

"Yes, you are MY director, Mr. Wild. When the audience is watching this film do you imagine they'll be saying, *What fabulous Continuity*? They'll be talking about *my* performance. They'll be discussing the great cast, the fantastic story, but they sure as hell won't be discussing *Continuity* over a glass of wine at dinner, trust me, unless of course, Cassandra fucks up, which I'm sure she *will* because she's only here because of you, not because she's dedicated to her job. Then you can watch *Skye's The Limit* on *The Worst Movie Mistakes of All Time* on YouTube and feel ashamed of yourself for having been such an unprofessional jerk! I want that woman gone by tonight. I want her on the next plane home to England where she belongs."

"Don't hold a gun to my head, Star. It doesn't become you."

"Oh yes, it does become me or I wouldn't be playing the role of Skye in the first place! Don't worry, Mr. Wild, if you won't fire her, I will." Star still had her hand on the trailer door, ready to make her exit.

"You just can't stand me having a girlfriend, can you? This has nothing to do with professionalism. You cannot control my life, Star. I'm your director, and you're a member of my cast. We had a little fun but you made it very clear what your limits are, and I respect that. You're young and vulnerable, and I simply won't take advantage. There are a lot of men out there who'd feed you bullshit—promise you all sorts of things just to fuck you and then they'd break your heart. I'm being honest. I'm twenty-six, I'm a bloody sex addict, for fuck's sake. I'm not going to offer you marriage and babies and spin you a yarn about how we're destined for each other, when I hardly even know you."

"Oh, you *know* me all right—we're cut from the same cloth. And you *do* want me: the whole goddamn package. You're just too much of a coward to admit it! Too weak to give yourself to me a hundred percent because you *know* you'd fall in love with me and lose control. In fact, you're *already* in love with me. Go ahead, fuck that skinny plain-Jane for all I care; it'll be *me* you'll be fantasizing about!" Star opened the door and stepped out of the trailer.

It was hard for me to admit, but what she was saying was close to the truth. "Star, this is ridiculous, please—"

She turned around and locked her eyes with mine. "You can call me *Miss Davis* from now on. I don't want you to speak to me unless you're directing me. Is that clear?" She slammed the door shut and was gone.

I'd direct her, alright. I needed her to do exactly as she was told, for once in her bloody life.

Before she took me over completely.

S HAKING, I PULLED OUT my cell from my prison uniform pocket and realized how ridiculous I must have looked just now, screaming at Jake in this hideous outfit and telling him how much he wanted me. *Not.*

"Brian," I said, hearing a wheeze at the other end of the line.

"Star, what a pleasure to hear your voice. What can I do you for?"

"I want the new Script Supervisor—the woman hired for Continuity—fired. *Now.*"

"The one replacing Susan while you're all in the Badlands? The English girl, Cassie?"

"Yes, her."

"She was the only person we could get last minute—Susan has a funeral to go to abroad. Cassie's filling in for a week."

"I want her *gone*, Brian. There's no telling what could happen otherwise."

"What are you saying, Star?"

"Rumor has it she does drugs." I knew I was being cruel but the words came flying out of my mouth.

He laughed raucously. I pictured his huge belly rippling with amusement—he was such a Hollywood producer cliché. "What, little Miss Perfect?" he said with a wheeze, chuckling as he spoke. "I doubt it."

"Just make it happen, Brian." I pressed END. I wanted to feel remorseful. It wasn't Cassie's fault and I was being a prime bitch. But it was true—I needed her *out of sight*. The idea of Jake touching her filled me with . . . fury . . . no . . . pain. Whatever it was, it made me nauseous.

I had to make him all *mine* or I'd go crazy.

I turned around and headed right back to his trailer. Some force was propelling me to do so, although I didn't know what I'd do when I got there, or what I'd say. Heat rose through me. I was shaking. Indignation. Fury. Revenge. Spite. I didn't bother to knock. I crashed through the door and was surprised that he wasn't sitting right there as he had been five minutes before. I could hear the shower going. I locked the door behind me so we wouldn't be disturbed, ready to give him more hell, and stomped over to the bathroom. I could smell lavender shampoo, or shower gel, which somehow calmed my senses. Then I observed his beautiful, lithe, strong body through the glass shower screen. He was covered in suds, the muscles in his arms flexed as he washed his hair—his stomach lean and hard. Anger morphed into desire and I found myself stripping off my prison costume, right there.

"Hello? Is someone there? Leo? Is that you?" shouted Jake over the rush of water.

I opened the glass accordion door and stood before him, naked. Water was gushing over his head, soap in his eyes, but he turned and squinted at me through the suds. I stepped into the shower and right into his strong arms. He held me close, gripping my body, flush against his.

"Miss Davis," he breathed into my ear, "what an amazing surprise." He pinned me against the wall and our mouths swooped together in a frantic rush of need and emotion. My tongue tangled with his; licking, lashing, sucking. I could feel his hardness press up against my stomach—his cock, huge—and I knew that this could be it. This could be the end of my virginity and I didn't even care anymore. I needed him. I wanted him. And I'd let him have me.

"Mr. Wild," I breathed into his mouth, "be my director. Tell me what to do."

"Oh baby," he said, "you bet I will."

PRODUCTION
Falling Star

DIRECTOR
Jake Wild

DATE
June

SCENE
Star's Blow job

TAKE
6

CAMERA
Jake Wild

JESUS I WAS HARD. If Star had been any other girl I would have fucked her arse off, right there. Her tits were round and shapely, all pretty curves and long legs, her tangled hair smoothing down her back with the rush of water, her makeup trickling down her face, streaks of colors—a rainbow running down her front, over her peaked, rosy nipples. I grabbed her worked-out butt, and drew her closer to me as I sucked her tongue and then bit her lower lip gently.

"Fuck, you're sexy," I groaned into her mouth, my hard-on pressing up against her taut stomach.

"All I think about twenty-four hours a day is fucking you, Star."

She drew out her tongue and licked along my lips. My cock flexed—all of me connected. I felt her slim hand take my throbbing erection, as the hot water gushed down on top of us. The heat, her touch, and my pounding desire had my head swooning. I steadied myself against the shower wall.

"It's huge," she panted, her mouth parted.

"Grip it hard, baby. Move your hand up and down."

She did as she was told and it thrilled me that she wanted to please me—tingles shot through my groin right down to my toes—my eyelids half-mast in ecstasy as her hand moved up and down from the root to the tip. "I want you to suck my cock, baby, can you do that for me?"

"It'll be a first," she said. Her eyes were wide and innocent, her full lips red and soft, and all I could think of was how great I'd feel inside her warm mouth. "But I want to try," she added.

"Bend down and take however much of me feels comfortable. If it's too much just lick it up and down. Like an ice cream or lollipop." The word 'lollipop' made me feel guilty. She was still a teenager and it probably hadn't been so long ago that she was licking *real* lollipops. Still, Dick was taking control of my brain and there was no turning back now. My brazen, unstoppable horniness was at the top of the Richter scale.

She knelt down, her wet hair flopping over her head as she tentatively licked the wide head of my cock. Her warm tongue flickered on my crown and I groaned loudly. I didn't want to force her or intimidate this little kitten. She needed to 'discover' me for herself. This was a big deal for a first-timer. I leaned back against the wall and flexed my hips up at her.

"Keep holding on to it, Star. Grip it hard at the base. Tight. Open your mouth and wrap your lips around it. See how huge and rock-hard it is? That's all for you, baby."

She didn't put my cock in her mouth as I'd suggested, but instead, started rimming my swollen crown with her tongue, around and around. I gripped my hand over hers and guided her up and down my cock, slowly at first but then faster and faster.

"Keep doing what you're doing Star, it feels fucking great." There was no way I'd ram myself inside her mouth now, nor push down her head, nor demand her to take me to the base of her throat. She was doing just great for a beginner and the last thing I wanted to do was put her off cocks for life by being a jerk. Just her lips on the tip of me was driving me nuts and I could feel the heat build in my groin as I guided her hand up and down, up and down the length of me.

Then she did something unexpected: she took my hand away, grabbed my arse, pulling me closer to her lips, and took most of my cock all the way inside her mouth. That was it. Within seconds I knew I'd explode—my warning last minute—last second. "I'm gonna come, Star—take your mouth away, baby, you may not like it."

But she sucked on me harder, her eyes closed tight in concentration.

I was groaning as I fucked her hot wet mouth, my fantasy coming true, although I felt bad for her—so many weeks of abstinence all exploding in her innocent, virgin mouth . . . "Star!" I yelled out, my orgasm intense, deep and mind-blowingly powerful. And then the last words in the world I wanted escaped from my lips—words I had no right to be saying: "I love you," I moaned. "I lo—" and I cut myself short, stopped myself from digging my grave any deeper than it already was.

THERE'S A FIRST TIME for everything, but I had never imagined I'd get so intimate with a man. Jake was huge and although I should have been intimidated by his size, I felt a raw fascination—giving him a blow-job was my way of getting closer to him. I began by just lightly kissing the tip of his erection, but before I knew it, a hunger arose in me; a hunger for power and control. This man was practically weeping with pleasure and it felt incredible.

That's why I took all of him in my mouth. He was in ecstasy, but at the same time, thoughtful on my behalf—not forcing me, not being the way I had imagined most men would be: overbearing, selfish and greedy. I felt special and revered and it made me want him more. And when he said, "I love you, Star," the moment was pure *magic*.

I licked off the last drops around my mouth, savoring the salty warmth that I'd avoided for so many years with other men, because the idea had grossed me out. I looked up through my wet lashes at Jake's beautiful firm stomach, to his magnificent chest, and finally to his eyes, half-closed, full of sex, lust, and most importantly, love.

"Star, that was incredible." He took me by the shoulders and raised me up to a standing position—the stretch felt good on my spine. I'd been crouched over him, the water beating down on us and hadn't realized in my moment of passion—that I'd been pretty uncomfortable. He turned me around so my back was to him and started massaging my hair with shampoo. Nobody had washed my hair since Mom and I'd forgotten how soothing it was; such a gentle gesture of care and love. Simple but pure—an unselfish act—washing someone else's hair. And boy, did my hair need some TLC after the prison scenes.

"You have such beautiful hair, Star."

I leaned against him—letting out a long sigh—and gave myself over completely as he massaged my scalp, his firm fingers strong and purposeful—kneading me. Needing me. In that moment I felt that Jake Wild was in love with Star Davis and that we would conquer any obstacles. His girlfriend blip would be rinsed away like the water cleansing off the suds from my hair—he'd laugh about Cassie being fired, and he'd be all *mine.* It was obvious by the way he touched me; rough enough to show me that I was his possession, and gentle enough to make me know that he'd do anything for me. He was still rock-hard—I could feel his rod against my butt and it was making my belly pool with longing. Jake trailed kisses along the nape of my neck, his thumbs making their way from my scalp downwards, pressing gently into the knotted muscles in my shoulders. I relaxed completely, giving myself over to him.

"You're so, so beautiful Star, you know that?" Jake breathed into my ear and his words shimmied through me like a soft breeze. He nipped my lobe and my body felt like it was on fire.

His deft fingers worked their way down my back to my waist, to the crease in my butt, brushing past the throbbing inside of my thighs— then they trailed back up to my waist, around my stomach and up to my breasts. I felt my nipples harden with the proximity of his large hands as he teased me—making circles around them; not touching my nipples. I groaned, heat pounding between my legs, silently willing him to do more. When he tweaked each nipple between his thumb and forefinger, tugging gently, a powerful tingle shot straight to my clit. I could sense my wetness—I was ready to let him take me. He was in love with me and that was all that mattered. He'd said the L word and I could feel the power of it in his touch—his need for me; the way he was worshipping my body.

Suddenly he spun me around so my back was against the shower wall, cool against the tiles, only the rising steam between us. He knelt down and sucked on a nipple, drawing it into his mouth, groaning—a feral sound coming deep within his throat, his Adam's apple pulsing with desire. I trailed my eyes from the taut flexing muscles of his abdomen to the wispy line of fine hair beneath his bellybutton that led to his enormous erection. I felt another surge of wetness in my pussy and an ache I had never experienced before, of wanting a man inside me.

"I'm going to tease your clit, baby—don't worry, I won't enter you yet."

All I could do was moan and he shut my whimpering sounds out with his mouth, his lips on mine, his tongue darting inside, muting my cries. His fingers slipped inside my wetness, one, then two, then three, his thumb circling my clit at the same time, and I writhed against the wall of the shower. He took his fingers out and popped them in his mouth, water gushing over both of us.

"Fuck, you tasty sex-kitten, you."

"Jake, I love what you do to me," I murmured, my eyelids fluttering in a carnal stupor.

He crouched down to my level, his legs planted wide, and gripping his huge erection guided it towards my opening. I moaned as he suddenly slapped me with his solid, thick cock. I pushed my hips at him. Then he slid his erection up and down my slit, careful not to enter me—

literally fucking my clit with his wide, velvety crown. All my emotions were locked between my thighs. Then he changed up the rhythm; slapped my entrance again—where every single cell of my body seemed to be gathered in a riotous clamor— then he drove his erection directly on my clit until I was seeing stars—I was going to come any second.

"I'm not going to fuck you here in the shower, Star. No, baby. I'm gonna make you come and then I'll take you to my bed where you can get on top of me and ride me."

He continued to slide his dick up and down my hard nub, every now and then entering me half a millimeter—enough to have every single sensation—pounding, throbbing, tingling, joining together in blissful harmony. I arched my back and gripped onto his shoulders as he continued his teasing, torturous pleasure of rimming, circling, pounding—using his rock-hard erection, not to get himself off, but to pleasure *me*. A live sex toy—it was driving me wild. Yes, "Wild."

"You can ride me when we're on the bed, Star, and control the pace yourself. Dip your hot, tight, pussy on the tip of my cock and let me stretch you open, little by little—your little virgin pussy can control the pace so you don't get split open by my size."

His dirty talk was really turning me on—the idea of pure pleasure mixed with a touch of pain had me gasping as he continued to fuck my clit. I could feel the build-up about to explode into a crescendo of emotion. He rammed me once more, and I felt myself coming hard. Really hard.

"Oh, Jake, oh my God!"

I was falling into a thousand pieces.

His mouth was on mine—my climax so intense, rushing through my whole core like a tsunami wave—out of control.

"Tell me you love me again," I said, urgency in my voice, gripping his scalp with my nails.

But he was silent—just kept kissing me like he hadn't heard.

"Say those words again you said earlier, Jake— tell me you love me." Another spasm of orgasm ripped right through me.

"Star, baby, I *care* for you," he whispered.

I was still coming but confused—my brain a

haze. "You said you loved me, Jake," I whispered back into his mouth.

He mumbled, "Really, did I?"

What?? What the hell game was he playing? I snapped back to Planet Earth—my climax after-shocks dying down, his new words a total 180 from twenty minutes before. "Jake you told me you *loved* me!"

His lips tilted into a smirk and he finally let go of his cock: the "tool" that had completely undone me and turned me into this vulnerable wreck.

"Star, baby, the first lesson any woman needs to learn is that if a man says he loves you while he's simultaneously coming, you shouldn't believe him." He winked at me as if what he'd said was cute and funny.

I pushed him off me—or tried to. He was strong. "What are you saying? That what you told me was *bullshit?*" I turned my head to the side so his lips were no longer on mine, and pressed my hands against his chest, attempting to lever him away from me.

"I must have meant them in the heat of the moment but—"

"You asshole!" I shrieked. "Get *off* me!"

"May I remind you that I was innocently having a shower and you stepped right in to join me, Star. Stripped naked and wanton—this was your idea, not mine."

I hated to admit it, but he was right. "Give me the conditioner and get out of the shower, *asshole*!"

He chuckled again, and kissed me on the forehead, not taking my tirade seriously. "This is *my* shower! *My* trailer," he said. "You're my guest."

"Then you should treat your guests with more courtesy. Just hand me some conditioner for my tangled hair and I'll be gone." My heart was pounding through my chest. Fury. Disbelief. But at the same time the most pronounced anger I had was toward myself. Jake Wild was a player. Everyone knew that. He himself had admitted he was a sex addict, and that I should keep well away from him. And most importantly of all: *Hellooo-o, Star?? What were you thinking? HE HAS A GIRLFRIEND!*

"I don't have any conditioner, I'm sorry," was all he said. Not, *Baby, I didn't mean it, of course I love you*, but sorry because he didn't have any goddamn conditioner?? ASSWIPE!!

"Get out of my way, you worthless piece of . . . of . . . director," I hissed at him, scrambling for the right words. "You're in the wrong profession, Jake. You should be an actor instead. You had me pretty convinced, earlier, that you had real feelings for me, but it was your *dick* that was talking, not you. I suppose I should thank you for at least being honest." I pushed him out of the way, shoved open the shower door and grabbed a towel. My hair was a matted mess—it was evident that, unlike his acting skills, his hair washing was less than professional. *Ugh*!

"Star, I never made you any promises— where's all this coming from? You knew the score. I thought you understood!"

"Oh I understand, alright. I understand loud and clear, that you're a two-timing jerk, that your ego is the size of the Empire State building, and that as long as you lie to women, you'll never find happiness. I've been a fool to come anywhere near you and I regret it." My words of irony hit me hard in the gut. "Come anywhere near"—yes, I'd *come*, alright. Big-time. And it had been the best sexual experience of my life. Tears welled in my eyes. He'd broken my heart with his *I love you* bullshit that I'd believed like the gullible fool I was. "This won't be happening again," I added bitterly, "I can guarantee you. I don't like liars."

"It wasn't exactly a lie," he said, trying to grab my wrist, but I shook him off—it was too late— the damage had been done.

I grabbed two more towels so there was nothing left for him to dry himself with, wrapped one around my hair, another over my shoulders, and one around my waist, and stormed out of his trailer, leaving my costume behind. We were done with the prison scenes—he could have my outfit as a memento of what a douchebag he'd been.

Mom was right. *Men, all of them . . . are LYING BASTARDS!* And I thanked my lucky stars (no pun intended) that my virginity was still intact. Close call.

A very, *very* close call.

PRODUCTION
Falling Star

DIRECTOR
. Jake Wild

DATE
. June

SCENE
Cock-teaser

TAKE
8

CAMERA
. Jake Wild

THAT WAS IT! That was the second and *last* time I'd fall for Star's prick-teasing game. What had I been *thinking*? Her cock-teasing had reached epic levels of professionalism. And each time I had fallen for it, hook line and sinker. I'd bloody well had enough!

I sat there humiliated, water dripping all over my trailer—Star had taken all the towels. I grabbed her T-shirt from the floor to dry myself but started swooning with the scent of her instead. Like Al Pacino in *Scarface* with his coke, I uncontrollably shoved my nose into the fabric that had been touching her skin and inhaled—her sweet sweat, her fragrance—and instantly missed her, my head spinning into a dreamy reverie and wishing I'd just gone along with the "love" story. Why not? Most men did that. Serial monogamy. Fucking one person after another, under the guise of seriously dating each partner in a "forever" relationship, every single time. People even did it with marriages. My dad, for instance. "Committing" a hundred percent, then bailing if it didn't work out. At least I was being honest.

Or was I?

I'd really bungled things. What had I been thinking getting Cassie involved? She was a sweet girl and didn't deserve this. I was using her for my own ends and I knew—breathing in Star's T-shirt once more—that having sex with Cassie would be like jerking off to a Playboy centerfold. I'd feel nothing except physical gratification. If I fucked Cassie my mind would be on Star. Was I in love with that prick-teasing bitch? I couldn't be—I hardly knew her! Yet I was obsessed with her. Possessed by her, and it was doing my head in. I needed to take my power back and be in control. I wasn't used to these feelings: my stomach like a cement mixer when she touched me, my brain a constant "Starry" Milky Way, thinking about her twenty-four-seven. I sat there, still wet, and fisted my hard cock, memory-flashes of it in her lush, warm mouth, her lips wrapped tightly around me, only twenty minutes before. I frantically jerked myself off, trying to find some relief, knowing that yes, actually—those words I said may well have been true: I was fucking well falling in love.

With a prick-teasing, manipulative, control-freak virgin:

Star bloody Davis.

I CAREENED STRAIGHT into Biff as I stomped away from Jake's trailer (okay, not really stomping as I was barefooted).

"Star, you'll catch a cold—let me take you home."

"Home?"

"Yes, back to Jake's. You're done shooting for the day." Biff knew my schedule better than I did.

"I need to go to my *own* home first," I said. "I need to see the contractor." I had no intention of ever going back to Jake's. So he could torment me with his 'real' girlfriend? Not a chance. I thought I could perhaps stay in the maid's apartment above my garage, as my house would be a dusty mess; if not, I'd come back to my trailer for the night—or a hotel—anywhere but Jake's.

Biff winced. "Sorry, Star. I can't do that. Jake would be furious with me—I could get fired. Unless Jake asks me directly, I would never go behind his back."

"Never mind, I'm going back to my trailer now to sort out my hair."

"Let me come with you." Her deep voice made me remember that she was a lesbian and I was clad only in towels. "I'm fine, Biff, I'll see you later."

Back in my trailer, I emptied half a bottle of conditioner on my hair and ran a comb through the knots. I had another shower and washed that lying son-of-a-bitch "right out of my hair," singing the song as I did so, and then flung on a long, flowing hippy dress. Nothing sexy or provocative, although I did put on black matching underwear and some black thigh-highs. Sexy underneath to make myself feel good, but chaste and pure on the outside—enough of this flirting game—it was landing me in trouble. No more games in general. The only person I was hurting was myself.

I called Janice.

"Hi Star, what's up?"

"Come and get me from the lot—I'll let them know at the gate you're arriving."

"Is everything okay?"

"No. I need to get the hell out of here and go home, but they're all spying on me. Maybe you can divert their attention and we can work out a plan." I heard a knock at my door. "Yes?"

"Star? It's me, John—just checking you're okay. Jake has instructed me to drive you home."

Big John the bodyguard. Jake's bodyguard who may have even been eavesdropping. Who knew? Maybe my trailer was bugged. "I'm busy right now," I shouted out—"hold on, Janice"—and then, "I'm about to take a shower, John."

"I'll be ready in fifteen minutes," John said.

"Make that one hour," I yelled through the door—"I want to go over my lines first."

"Okeydokey, I'll be right here, waiting outside."

Waiting outside? Was he just going to sit there without budging? I needed to escape, go to my house—there was no way I'd spend the night at

Jake's, with or without my own bed. Biff could sadly not be bribed—well, *maybe* I could have pushed her, but poor thing, it wouldn't be fair. There was no way Big John would let me waltz off with Janet. I called Leo on my cell. Jake trusted him.

"Leo," I said sweetly.

"What's up, babe?" he said, in his thick Russian accent.

"Are you still here on the lot?"

"Sure am, what can do you for?" I loved the way he got expressions slightly wrong.

"I don't want Big John to drive me to Jake's."

"Why not?"

"Because," I whispered, "at times he looks at me in a . . ." I tried to come up with an adjective that wasn't too incriminating—"in a flirtatious manner and I don't feel comfortable with him."

"I talk to Jake—this is bullshit—he's your bodyguard!"

"He's not my real bodyguard. My guys have been put on hold for the duration of the movie— the producers didn't trust them—wanted to hire their own."

"So what do you want me to do? Tell Jake?"

"No, don't say a word—and please don't mention what I said about Big John to anybody, I don't want him to lose his job. All I want is for you to drive me to my house."

"Your house has builders, no? Under construction?"

"It's being remodeled. I want to go and talk to the contractor."

"It's six p.m., Star, I doubt he'll be there, still."

"Please, Leo."

"Okay. I'll call Jake,"

"No!"

"Star, I have to ask Jake first. He's my boss. Could lose job."

I groaned. This was a nightmare!

"Look, I'll call him on my other cell right now."

"He'll say no, Leo."

"I'll handle it. I can be your bodyguard, just for today."

PRODUCTION
Falling Star

DIRECTOR
- Jake Wild

DATE
- June

SCENE
Cassie's tears

TAKE
10

CAMERA
- Jake Wild

C ASSIE SAT THERE in my trailer, tears in her eyes. I felt like such a bastard, but what could I do?

"First finding out I'm off the job and now this," she sniveled—"this whole trip has been such a waste of time, not to mention mind-fuck, Jason."

I held her hand. I was still wet from the shower. "I'm sorry, Cass, Brian said it was a union thing. They had to have someone *union*. I have no idea why they didn't second guess that. I'm sorry you're off the job."

"Well obviously you're not sorry or you

wouldn't be sending me home!"

"There's no point you coming all the way to the Badlands to twiddle your thumbs, with nothing to do except stare at the scenery all day."

"It's about *us*, Jason, not the bloody job. You wrote me such a beautiful email. I really believed you wanted to make it work between us. 'Two minds alike,' you said, 'two needs make one whole', you said."

I bowed my head in shame. Unpardonable behavior—messing with her heart like this. "I'm sorry, Cass."

"You said it was what you wanted."

"I did want it, Cass. I swear I did. But we're such old friends it—"

She waved away my excuse. "You just don't fancy me. Course you don't. Why would you when you've got beautiful babelicious starlets waiting in the wings?—just that . . . well . . . I thought you'd grown out of that and wanted a *real* relationship based on more than just sex."

"You deserve better than me, Cassie. Far better. I'd probably be unfaithful." *Probably. What a joke.* I wondered if she could smell Star on me now. I was no good for any woman, least of all someone like Cassie, who was pure and good, kind and honest. "Cass, about that flat in London—the loft you went to see in Bow that you said you liked . . . I'll buy it for you."

Cassie's mouth pressed into a tight hard line. Then she said, "I don't want your money, don't you *get* that?"

"You're one of my oldest friends, Cass. Friends help each other out. I want to do this for you. It would make me feel better."

"It's always about *you* and what *you* want, isn't it? You can't buy love and friendship, least of all as a way to alleviate your crap behavior."

"I'm sorry, Cass, I just want to try to make it up to you somehow."

"You're phone's ringing. Pick it up," she said.

"It can wait," I answered quickly, the bastard in me trying to give her some respect. This "break-up" before we'd even "made-up" was ridiculous—the poor woman had only just arrived in LA. My eyes cut a glance at Cassie's face; her slim lips, her too short hair, and I secretly wished that she were Star. That Star was the "good girl" who'd save me from my philandering ways, who'd rescue me from myself. I wished that, somehow, Star and I could make it work.

"Pick your bloody phone up—if you don't, I will," Cassie barked.

I was still wet. Naked, Star's T-shirt covering my crotch, hoping Cassie wouldn't notice Star's prison uniform and her panties tossed on the floor. The panties that I'd probably take to bed with me later.

Cassie slid the buzzing phone across the table at me. I looked at it. It was Leo. "What?" I said. "Make this quick."

"Star wants to go home," he said down the line.

"So let her go—she's done for the day." Star, Star, Star! Her name was driving me fucking crazy. What sort of a name was Star, anyway? I didn't even know her real name and here I was obsessing about her. Bloody prick-teaser! Heat rolled through my gut in a nauseous wave. Fury. Despair. Horniness. Desperation. "Look, Leo, I don't have time for this—you *deal* with it."

"But she doesn't want John—"

"Make an executive decision, for fuck's sake it. *You* deal with her, I'm busy!" I pressed the red button, cutting Leo short. Cassie deserved better than to sit here listening to Star Davis's whims and fancies. "Sorry, Cass, where were we?"

But it was too late. I followed Cassie's gaze to where Star's prison uniform lay on the floor, together with her ivory silk panties.

"What was I thinking?" Cassie said, a fresh tear sliding down her cheek, her eyes fixed on the flimsy knickers that were an excuse for underwear. "I must need my *head* examined. So dumb! I'm such an idiot! Why did I fall for your *bullshit*, Jason?" She stood up, stared at me for a second and then slapped me hard across the face. I felt a ringing in my left ear and a sharp sting, almost relishing the pain.

"Go ahead, Cass, do it again, or *punch* me this time, I deserve it—go on. Punch me in the face, it'll make you feel better." I meant what I said. I sat there, helplessly clutching Star's T-shirt to my groin, but not being able to chase after Cassie— naked as I was—as she stormed out of my trailer yelling:

"You selfish *arsehole*! You know what? You need psychiatric help. You will never be happy until you cure your sex addiction."

Her prophecy was right. I reflected on my shitty ways for a second and felt like a victim of my manhood. *Men are wired this way. Eyes > brain > dick . . . or . . . brain > eyes > dick. Bypassing higher centers of reason.* Or maybe it was Star's smell. Whatever, she had a hold on me. She'd intoxicated me—bewitched me, even. I wanted to control my one-track mind but I couldn't. I felt so bad for Cassie, but all I could think about was Star. Until she was completely mine, I knew I'd go insane.

"I need a SAA meeting," I muttered to myself, getting up and grabbing some gym clothes out of a duffle bag. "I need to go running and share—get my sorry arse under control. Or rather, Dick Bastardly under control."

I'D SEEN CASSIE bounce into Jake's trailer earlier like she owned it, and that was all I needed to compound the humiliation I felt, and the fiery anger that had been building up since he and I parted ways. She was his *girlfriend,* and I was the piece of fluff on the side—luckily I'd put a stop to things before Humiliation, with a capital H, could take hold completely.

Jake Wild was a self-centered, egomaniac who got his thrills by having multiple women in love with him at one time. He needed his ego massaged daily to make himself feel special. Why I had fallen for his charms, I had no idea, when it was obvious he would *never* change. He was a damaged Hollywood casualty and, of all people, I should have known better than to play with faulty goods.

Leo was driving as I sat in the front seat of the studio car with my bare feet on the dashboard, singing along to the music. Ironically it was that song, "A Sky Full Of Stars" by Coldplay. Skye full of stars. Skye/Star—it was if we were interchangeable. I wanted to think that Jake saw me as a sky full of stars, thinking only of me and his movie—his movie and me—but I knew that wasn't so and took a deep breath, willing my wishful fantasy away.

"So Jake didn't even care, huh?" I asked Leo, "didn't mind that I wasn't going home with John?"

"He was busy. Irate. Told me to make executive decision. I thought we could have bite to eat, Star. Are you hungry?" He turned to me and flashed his Russian megawatt smile, accompanied by a wink.

"Sure," I said. I *was* hungry, as it happened— eating had been the last thing on my mind earlier, when I was focused on shooting such an intense scene.

Leo had one hand on the steering wheel and his elbow casually on the sill of the open window. A cool breeze filled the smooth-sailing, shiny black Lexus, as it hummed along La Cienega Boulevard, and whipped his dark, floppy hair away from his face. His shirtsleeves were rolled up and revealed, on one forearm, a bear, and on the other, a symbol, but the tattoo was badly done—homemade.

"What's that tat?" I asked.

"Which one? I have so many."

"The blurry one on your arm with the bluish ink—I can't make out what it is."

"Nothing you need to know about," he said with an enigmatic smile. He'd piqued my curiosity.

"You did it yourself?"

"No."

"If you decided to get a tattoo, why didn't you go to a professional?"

He laughed. "I didn't decide, Star. It wasn't like that."

"Tattoos," I said, "are always a choice—maybe a bad one, but—"

"Oh are they now." It wasn't a question but a

statement. "What food are you in mood for?" he asked, changing the subject. "Oh yes, I remember, no meat, etcetera. There's a place nearby where they sell Middle Eastern stuff—take-out, but good. You like falafel, pita bread, hummus?"

"Sounds perfect." I glanced at the tautly strung tendons in his forearm again, where the smudgy tattoo lived. His muscles flexed as he maneuvered the car around a bend. There was something rough and raw about Leo. Not like Jake, who was classy—no, Leo was rugged and could have easily passed for my bodyguard. I guessed that's why they had let him take me home—because he could have punched out anyone, done some damage; except he wasn't carrying arms, of course. At least, I didn't think so, although he did look the type to have a Colt.45 stuffed behind the waistband of his jeans.

"What's your story, Leo?"

A ghost of a smile flickered on his lips. "It's a long one—maybe some other day."

"Family?"

"Kind of."

I laughed. "Yeah, that's how I feel." I put my

feet higher up on the dashboard and noticed him flick his glimmering green eyes at the bit of my exposed thigh where my dress had risen up, revealing the top of my stocking. Then he forced his gaze back to the road ahead.

"What brought you to LA?" I asked.

"Jake Wild."

"Sorry, that was a dumb question. I forgot he discovered you from that film school competition in London. "So that's what took you to London—you got a place to study film?"

"No, my uncle had a job for me in London. But soon as I had money saved I went to film school—got hell away from job."

"That bad, huh? What was the job?"

"Nothing good."

"Waiting tables?"

"No, nothing respectable like that."

"Some kind of menial job? Flipping burgers or something?"

"Had to pay back debt doing some—"—he cut himself off mid-sentence. "Please, Star, don't ask me about my past—it's not pretty." He cracked his knuckles, and I suddenly got the

picture: Leo was a knuckle-cracking kind of guy.
No way had he been flipping burgers; his job must
have been something far more underground. Dark.
Dangerous. His tattoos spoke a thousand words.
Not like Jake's lion tattoo; beautifully executed,
artistic, with a myriad of colors and attention to
detail. No, Leo's told a different story—what that
story was, I wanted to find out.

"So you're close to your uncle?" I asked,
hoping for a clue.

"Last I heard, something went down and he
got shot," Leo said, with no emotion whatsoever.

"I'm sorry," I offered, tentatively.

"I'm not." He swerved the car suddenly into a
parking lot. "Here we are, Star. You wanna wait in
the car? while I get take-out? Or we could eat
inside restaurant."

"Is it busy? I don't want to end up signing
autographs all evening."

"Wait here. I'll be right back."

I watched him edge his tall, solid frame out of
the car and swagger purposefully toward the
restaurant. He turned and zapped the locks on the
car with the remote. A nice attention to detail.

Protective. I felt safe with Leo and wished he were my bodyguard for real. There was something erotic about a man who would lay down his life for you—protect you under any circumstance. My bodyguards, and John—the one they'd hired for me especially for the movie—were hardly eye-candy like Leo, though.

I observed him as he held the restaurant door open for two teenage girls as they came out. They began giggling at his gallant gesture, practically swooning as if they'd seen a rock star. I'd noticed that about him; he held doors open for women and stood up whenever anyone of the opposite sex came into the room, or got up from the table to go to the bathroom when we were in a restaurant. Unusual, especially for a man of our generation.

A diamond in the rough.

I heard the girls squeal at each other excitedly. I buzzed my passenger seat back, fiddled with the radio station and lay back, stretching out my legs. I'd have a quick shut-eye, I decided—filming, and all the Jake drama, had made me tired, especially when I reminded myself of what a dumb-ass I'd been, fooling around with a man who had a girlfriend. A movie director, no less. What a Hollywood cliché. Yes, I was exhausted and felt my heavy eyelids close as Jhené Aiko's "The Worst" floated in my subconscious.

I AWOKE WITH A JOLT and observed a solid pair of legs standing there beside the passenger door. Leo leaned in and put the take-out bags on the floor in front of me.

"Sleeping Beauty," he said in a low, quiet voice. "Sorry to wake you, Star."

I put my hand over my mouth and yawned.

"There was line, sorry I took so long." He leaned in closer and I could feel his breath on my face. He smelled of mint and some faint—very faint—earthy, manly scent, like the woods in spring after a heavy bout of rain. I thought for a second that he was going to kiss me, but he was just buckling up my seat belt.

"Oh, my God!!" It *is* her. It *is* her! It's Star Davis! I told you so!"

I flicked my eyes up and saw a bevvy of teenage girls and a couple of young guys honing in on us, their Smartphones pointed through the open car door. Leo snapped to attention, closed the door shut and stood there, blocking me from our new audience. Luckily, the car had tinted windows, but they'd already gotten their shot, or worse, mini movie. He quickly dashed around to his side, leaped into the car, and we screeched off.

"Pain in neck, must drive you crazy," he said, shaking his head with annoyance.

"I'm used to it. Wanna be my new, full-time bodyguard?" I half joked.

"Not chance in hell. I'd lose my temper, probably." We shot out of the parking lot, people's iPhones pointing at the back of the car.

"This is being fed to YouTube or Tweeted right now, guaranteed," I said. "Step on it before they follow us."

"Where are we going?"

"I live in Hancock Park."

"Hand Cock? Love the name," Leo said with a smirk.

"I know, right?" I dug a soda out of one of the

take-out bags, popped the ring, stuck in a straw and took a sip. "But my neighborhood is very old-fashioned. Big old mansions, with huge backyards for people's 2.5 kids. It was designed and built in the 1920s and it hasn't changed much since. It's a historical neighborhood." I handed Leo my can of Coke but he didn't want any.

"Not usual sort of place for young movie star," he said.

"That's why I chose it. I just want a discreet, normal life, you know?"

"2.5 kids?"

"One day, yeah."

"Me too."

"Really? *You*? You're kidding me."

"Why so surprised? I had troubled childhood. Want to make it right. Even guys like me with badass tattoos have dreams, right?"

We drove along in silence and I ruminated on Jake and felt bad for him that he didn't seem to want the good things in life. Family. Kids. A stable life. Or if he did, he didn't want those things with *me* but with someone like boring, squeaky-clean *Cassie*. I thought about Mindy and wondered if

Leo would be a good match for her, now that I realized he wasn't the player I had imagined him to be. Or maybe he was. Maybe his 2.5 kids fantasy was just talk. Men love to do that. Get women's hopes up, just to get them into bed. Leo's, "How loud will you scream when I fuck you?" when we first met hadn't worked, so now he was trying a new, more subtle tactic. Smart.

We finally arrived at my house, a Spanish Colonial, approximately ten thousand square feet of pure Heaven, with six bedrooms, nine bathrooms, and an office, on a double corner lot of nearly an acre. Right now, the roof was being fixed, and I was converting the loft into an extra room. I couldn't wait to get back. It had a theater room in the den with a state-of-the-art movie projector and screen. Next to it: a bar (now stocked with only sodas and Perrier water). The dining room was wood paneled with a butler's pantry. There was even a wine cellar, and a kitchen that was the size of most people's whole apartments. The garden behind (I didn't call it a "back yard" because it was so much more) was landscaped, with fountains and perfectly trimmed box-hedges. A sparkling, mosaic-tiled pool with spa and a pergola, sat in the middle, and at the front, at the side of my house, a three-car garage, with a two-bedroom apartment above, where my full-time maid lived. I buzzed open the security gates and as we drove into the curving driveway, even *I* took a breath at its beauty (despite the temporary scaffolding), and when I cut a glance at Leo, he looked stunned.

"All this and you're only . . . how old?" he said, his green eyes wide.

"Nineteen. I know, it's pretty awesome." I was thinking of my next move—my plan to stay here and shake Leo off, or persuade him somehow, that we didn't need to go back to Jake's. "Come, I'll show you around," I said. But before I could get out of the car Leo had raced around to my door and opened it. And then, something happened: he came crashing down on me as if he'd had a sudden stroke: his head knocking against the edge of the car rooftop as he practically landed on my lap. That's when I too, blanked out.

Everything went black.

PRODUCTION
Falling Star

DIRECTOR
Jake Wild

DATE
June

SCENE
Staff meeting

TAKE
12

CAMERA
Jake Wild

M Y PULSE SPED UP as I mentally prepared my speech, but what came out was a garbled mess. "There's something about this girl," I started, "that makes me . . . literally crazy. Obsessed! I can't control myself. Which makes me feel it must be wrong, right? I mean, love is meant to be sweet and thoughtful and caring . . . but this girl, I almost want to throttle her . . . she drives me so . . . crazy! And then the drug feeling comes back. Full on. But it's not drugs I crave, but her." I was sweating. Had come straight here on my run and was donned in shorts and sneakers, probably stinking of B.O., but I did feel better after expending so much pent-up energy. I needed the exercise.

"It works if you work it," someone said, and then they all chanted, "Thanks for sharing, Jason."

I wanted to go on, but a bodybuilder in a wife-beater tank piped up: "I relapsed last night. Fucked two women in a row. One after the other. I picked the first one up at the gym, took her out and then got sidetracked by another, prettier one I met at the bar. I feel bad, man, like a real jerk. And the sex wasn't even that good. Worse, I didn't use protection."

The group nodded knowingly. But I felt sick hearing everyone else's sordid details. Star was different. Star was beautiful. Divine. Special. I felt I'd sullied her in some way, sharing details about her with strangers. I needed to get the hell out of this dirty meeting and see her in person. Tell her I wanted to make a go of it. A real relationship. Flowers, dinners. The whole damn lot. I needed to know if it was love I felt or simply lust, and the only possible way of finding out for sure was to woo her.

The old fashioned way.

I slipped out of the meeting but, with my head in my hands, went careening into someone glued to her iPhone. We were both at fault. "Sorry," we both said simultaneously.

I looked up. "Holly?"

"Jake, what a coincidence!" Then she furrowed her brows. "I came to this branch because I though I was being incognito." She laughed.

"Me too," I admitted. We'd both been caught.

"So, how's it going with *Skye's The Limit?*"

"Great," I told her. "How are things working out with my uncle? Is he treating you nicely?"

"He's a dream," she answered with a grin. I'd gotten Holly the job. I'd fucked her and then felt guilty: a sort of severance pay. "How about that wild child, Star Davis?" she went on. "You've got a lot on your plate with her."

"She's fine, really," I said, wishing I could have some sort of anonymity in this bloody town.

"I see she's having some fun with your AD?" Holly said with a little smirk.

"*What?*"

She shoved her iPhone in my face. "Twitter feed. That's why I crashed into you. This one's trending as we speak."

I looked at the screen. There was Leo, his lips centimeters away from Star's face, as Star gazed at him with her big fucking baby-doll blue eyes. My heart began to pound uncontrollably.

"Eat-A-Pita parking lot, couldn't keep their hands off each other apparently. Sexy guy your AD. When she's done with him, pass him my way."

I stood there, dumbfounded. Star was punishing me. Or maybe not. Maybe she genuinely didn't give a damn. And as far as Leo was concerned? He was fucking well fired. And if I had my way he'd never work in this town again. Dammit, I'd trusted him! I'd told him Star was off limits! But then, poor guy, as far as he knew I was still with Cassie. And it had been my own bloody fault that he was chaperoning Star home in the first place! No, I wouldn't fire him, but . . .

"Well, bye, Jake, see you around. Good luck with that little vixen. Rumor has it she's tipped to win an Oscar—great performance they're all saying. Early days though, eh? If she's hanging out with a Russian they're big on vodka shots and partying hard—"

"Bye, Holly," I interrupted. "Say hi to my uncle for me—tell him I'll call him soon."

I'd left my phone behind so couldn't call Leo. Bastard! I had to stop them! Right now!

I started running faster than I'd ever run in my life.

13.
Star

I OPENED MY EYES, expecting to find light, but stared into the unending darkness. I caught my breath, panicked by the eerie silence and deep black that was now my vision. I had no idea what time it was, nor where the hell I was. Some kind of bedding was beneath me. It was pitch, pitch black. My head felt groggy and I ached, but not with a headache when you have a pain behind your eyes from too much alcohol or something, but a hazy, flu-like feeling, thick in my brain. I tried to recall something—anything—but all that came to mind was the fact that I must be late and I should be on set.

That's right—I remembered suddenly—we'd be flying out early to South Dakota. My hands padded out in front of me and I felt an unfamiliar, hard mattress beneath me, some rough sheets, and I realized I was shivering. I pulled the sheet up around myself and felt my naked body, although I still had my bra, panties, and thigh-highs on. The mattress was directly on the floor. I walked my fingers to the edge of the bedding and felt the tackiness of linoleum. I tried to lift up my head and sit.

My lids felt heavy, swollen, and my head and shoulders slumped back down in a thud. I felt numb again and let myself fall back into a muzzy, dazed sleep.

THEY'D BEEN GONE for twelve hours. No news. Disappeared into thin air. The more I was finding out, the more painful their betrayal was. Star betraying her profession, and Leo betraying me. I'd given him a chance. Plucked him from obscurity. Star was being given a chance, too, by the studio—the role of a lifetime—and she was throwing it all away. For what? So we had a little scene in my trailer?—she got pissed off at me. So, what? It was no reason to bail on the movie *itself*. I still couldn't believe what they were telling me was true. Something didn't add up.

Brian poured us out another coffee. It was six a.m. We were in my kitchen, waiting for more news from the private investigators I'd hired. The Law wasn't taking this seriously as a "missing persons" case. Star had done this sort of thing before. Besides, it was their right, as adults, to do whatever they liked. Why would they waste taxpayers' money hunting down a runaway couple "in love?"

The ten-second YouTube video clip played over and over in my mind. Leo leaning in and saying, "Sleeping Beauty" and Star's eyes half-mast, full of lust, or full of something.

Brian was still talking—I was only half paying attention; my mind was focused on losing Star to Leo.

He rambled on, " '*So they broke their contracts, then 'sue them,*' a police officer said to me, thinking he was being smart. The law doesn't give a fuck, Jake. You did the right thing to hire private investigators—the cops aren't going to lift a finger to help us. They have gang shootings in South Central—a runaway movie star and her side-kick are the least of their problems."

I looked at my watch again. We should have been at the airport by now, settling into our cabins later this morning, and setting up shots for the golden hour, this evening, when we'd be commencing the car chase.

"It's just not like Star," Brian repeated for the umpteenth time.

"How do you know, what is, or isn't, 'like Star' " I snapped. "She's an alcoholic/drug addict, Brian—she's done this sort of shit before."

"No she hasn't, Jake. She may have turned up sozzled on set, but she still *showed*. She's a professional. 'The show must go on' . . . that's the kind of person she is. She wouldn't simply bail on her job like this, whatever personal problems she's having."

"I can't get over *Leo*," I muttered. "How could he do that to me? After all I've done for him?"

"Come on, Jake! He's an opportunist. A poor boy from Russia—"

"Ukraine, not Russia, there's a difference, Brian."

"Not really. You can't fool me that it should

be part of Europe with all this European Union crap. It's still got the Iron Curtain mentality—their people are half starving to death. Underprivileged is the same the world over, especially in the East. A poor, working class boy, that's Leo. Criminal record, you told me. Jailbird. Served time. Star has *money*. She's beautiful. He must have thought all his Christmases had come at once, dollar signs flashing in his eyes."

I longed to explain to Brian that it was *me* she'd been with, *me* she desired, but I didn't want to give him the pleasure of saying, "I told you so" and that it was my fault for fooling around with such a vulnerable teenager, fresh out of rehab, and I'd brought this upon us all. Besides, Brian was right. And maybe the Cassie stuff had really got to Star. Perhaps Star's feelings were genuine for me and I'd hurt her quite badly. But then the vision of Leo and her, as good as kissing, sent another fresh spike of jealousy ripping through my veins—I could feel the tightness of my mouth, my fists clenched—I wanted to punch somebody. I wanted to punch my own reflection in a mirror. I'd fucked up. Big time.

Brian went on, "Both their passports are with them, or at least missing, so they must have taken them. Suitcases packed, with clothing also missing—all this confirmed by Star's assistant, Janice—and Star's Porsche gone. You think maybe they decided to go on ahead of us to the Badlands?"

"If so, her Porsche would have been parked at one of the airports. Unless they decided to take a road trip and join us in a few days' time. Do some sightseeing in Mount Rushmore, or the Black Hills, or something."

"But Star knew we were meant to be shooting this evening—she wouldn't just not show."

"But their phones were left behind, Brian. Left on Star's kitchen table. That spells abandonment to me. They've scarpered off somewhere to be together. I just don't *get* it, though. So fucking *unprofessional.*"

"That's what I'm saying, Jake. Leo? yes. Star? Not a chance. She's been in this business from the age of two. *The show must go on*—that's every actor's mantra. It's part of an actor's DNA. Come rain or shine, no actor worth his or her weight abandons a project midway. It's like a sailor with his ship. There are unspoken rules. This just doesn't make sense."

"So what do we do now?"

Brian shrugged. He was chewing Juicy Fruit and drinking coffee at the same time. "Shoot around her? That's what Pearl Chevalier wants us to do. Use the stuntwoman we hired and a double for the car chase and wait until Star shows to do the close-ups and two-shots. Maybe she's just gone AWOL for twenty-four hours. Needs to clear her head. Who knows? But we have a lot of money at stake here, Jake. Payrolls, unions—I just don't think we can persuade the insurance to cover this. It isn't an 'accident' or anything. We're in a fix—a weird predicament. That's why a bodyguard was hired especially to watch her—" he raised his bushy eyebrows at me—"so this sort of thing wouldn't happen. I think all we can do is keep the investigators on it—see if they can track them down, which won't be easy without their cell phones acting as GPSs—and wait until she calls."

"*If* she calls," I mumbled. Guilt gathered thick in my throat. It was my fault that John had been given the go-ahead to let Leo drive Star back to my place. He probably wouldn't have agreed had he not seen Cassie in floods of tears, begging him to take her to the airport, and flinging her arms about his bear-like body—a damsel in distress. She'd wanted to get away from me as soon as possible, so when he called my cell I told him yes, to take Cassie to the airport—to book her into First Class—use the company credit card, which I'd pay back, and to give her whatever cash he had—I'd pay that back too—and yes, that it was fine for Leo to accompany Star home. But "home" turned out to be Star's house, not mine, where she'd planned her getaway.

What a fucking fiasco.

15. Star

'**D**O YOU KNOW that there are more stars than all of the grains of sand put together in the whole wide world?"

I finish braiding my Barbie's hair and look up from where I am on the trailer floor. I see a pair of dirty knees. His boot is planted right on top of Ken's face.

"Just goes to show how common stars are. Nothing special. Your new name is dumb. You're dumb."

"Please get your big ugly boot off of Ken's face," I say.

"Ken's gay, don't you know that? He's fucking your boy teddies behind dumb bitch Barbie's back."

"He is not."

"He is too."

I push my brother's pale, freckly leg away—or I try—but he squishes his foot harder into Ken's beady eyes, and his plastic head pops right off. Mom had gotten me Ken and Barbie from Goodwill—I wanted to give them a forever home, another chance, some love—and now look. I can feel a tear threatening to fall, but I won't cry. Not in front of HIM.

"I'm telling Mom you cussed," I tell my brother.

He laughs at me, his turned-up, piggy nose scrunching. "Fuck, fuck, FUCK. She won't hear you 'cos she's sleeping. Taken some blue ones."

"Get away from me, Travis. I wanna be alone."

"You're a spoiled little brat, you know that, Diane. Die Anne. I wish you would. I wish you'd just go and DIE so me and Dad can live in peace."

I WOKE UP WITH A JOLT—my dream having given me a clue. "Travis?" I shouted out. "Where am I?" But all I heard was silence ringing in my ears. My head was still heavy, and I sensed a bruise on the right side of my neck. I heaved myself up but fell straight back down, so I crawled on my hands and knees until I felt, not the mattress beneath me, but the linoleum floor. I smelled food, like the food Leo bought yesterday/today? I had no concept of time. It was the hummus, and it reminded me that we never ate, and my stomach was rumbling with hunger, but I also smelled a whiff of bleach—the two smells were somehow intermingled.

"Hello?" I screamed out as loudly as I could. "Is anybody there?"

I heard a low groan coming from the corner of the space—the room—wherever I was. The blackness was engulfing me. Still pitch dark. I couldn't make anything out. "Leo?"

Another groan.

I managed to crawl until I felt a wall, and I scrambled to my feet, walking and feeling the wall at the same time. My hands frantically paced up and down—hoping to find a light switch somewhere. Then I heard a siren in the distance; my ears becoming accustomed to the tiniest sound, and something made me suspect that we were high up, in a skyscraper, perhaps. I could make out the lonely drum of traffic, maybe twenty floors below.

"Star, is that you?" It was Leo, his voice a muffle, followed by another groan like he was in pain.

"Leo, I can't see you. Are you okay?" I wanted to rush to him, to the sound of his voice but my legs were weak, and I knew I'd collapse without the wall to hold me up.

"I think I'm okay," he moaned. "Where are we?"

I continued to shuffle my way around the edge of the room, feeling the wall as I went. It had the same kind of surface as piano practice rooms. Soundproofed. Plywood, with little holes to bounce the sound back. Finally, I felt something. I flicked up a switch and fluorescent light flooded the room.

Leo cried out, the flash of light obviously blinding him. "Ah, Jesus, like when I came out of cell to outside."

"Sorry." *Cell?* Had he been in prison? I covered my hands over my eyes to stop the dazzling glare. After thirty seconds or so, I peaked out, letting light seep between my fingers—my vision had just about adjusted itself. We were in an empty office space. Black paper had been duct taped over the windows. The door was next to me. No handle. Also soundproofed. The room was bare except a double mattress, and in one corner was another door—perhaps it led to a bathroom because it *did* have a handle. Leo was doubled-up in another corner, clutching his belly as if in pain. No blood, thank God. He was naked except for his boxer briefs. More of those smudgy tattoos decorated his chest and biceps. He looked out of place—such a tough-looking guy in a position of vulnerability. I felt a pang in my solar plexus. A longing to hold him and tell him everything would be all right.

But it wasn't alright. Not by a long shot.

I started to rush toward him, but my legs gave way and I fell down, smack on the floor. Rather than try to get up, I crawled forward and, like curious babies wanting to check each other out, he and I both made our way over to each other on our hands and knees. I practically crashed into him, wrapped my arms around his neck, tears stinging my eyes.

"I'm so sorry," I said.

He held me close and I felt momentarily safe in his strong grip, although I knew I wasn't. Our situation was terrifying. Both of us alone. Naked. Bruised.

But it could have been worse: at least we had each other.

For now, anyway.

He kissed my forehead and kept me clutched in his embrace. "Why sorry, Star? What fuck happened?"

"I don't know. We were in the Lexus, in the driveway at my house, and then I blanked out. But I have an idea. It's him; I *know* it is."

"Who?" he asked, weakly.

"Travis, my step-brother. He wants to punish me. This is just the kind of thing he'd do."

My eyes slid to that door again. I wriggled out of Leo's arms and crawled along the floor. "I'm hoping that's a bathroom," I said. "I need to pee."

It was. There was a basic shower, a toilet, and a sink. And, a mirror. I caught a glimpse of my reflection and shuddered. There was a massive bruise on my neck and dried blood that looked like a hickey. I'd been jabbed with a needle. Yeah, that made sense. That fucker's favorite TV show was *Dexter*. Travis had injected us with some knock-out drug, Dexter-style. What was it that Dexter used on his victims? Travis once told me. Etorphine? Enough to knock out an elephant. Immobilize even the most dangerous animals. Vets used it. That explained why Leo had been rendered immobile and unconscious—instantly. The only chance Travis had of knocking out a guy as big and strong as Leo. I'd been waiting for something like this to happen—hence my bodyguards— although I hadn't imagined a scenario such as this. It wasn't the public who I'd feared but my psychotic stepbrother, who'd had it in for me the moment he'd set eyes on me when I was five years old. He was nine at the time. Not much of a difference now, but a four-year gap was a lot between young siblings then.

Asshole.

I turned on the faucet and rinsed my face with cold water. And glugged down several mouthfuls—I was thirsty. There was a bar of soap and a couple of towels. A tube of toothpaste too, and a couple of brand new toothbrushes in their packaging. Travis's idea of generosity probably. I slumped down on the toilet seat, pulled down my panties, and let a rush of urine flood out. I flushed the toilet, but simply sat there, my weary, aching head propped up by my hands, my elbows resting on my knees. I was exhausted.

"You okay, Star?" I heard Leo call out.

No, I wasn't okay. Everything good in my life had come to an abrupt end. "Sure," I yelled back through the closed door, tears welling in my eyes, wondering what Travis's end game would be. Did he want me, literally, dead? or did he have some kind of ransom in mind?

The worst thing of all was . . .

Nobody knew we were here.

PRODUCTION
Falling Star

DIRECTOR
- Jake Wild

DATE
- line

SCENE
Pearl's call

TAKE
16

CAMERA
- Jake Wild

S TILL NO WORD. I couldn't concentrate. Six more hours had gone by and we had arrived at our cabins in the Badlands. There was no way I'd be able film anything, let alone shoot Star's double, who had been hired at the last minute. She didn't look like Star up close, but she had the same build, hair, and skin-tone—everything to make you do a double take (no pun intended) and make me believe that Star had returned to the set. A momentary blip. A mini relapse, perhaps. But, no. Star was good and gone, and by now, I was no longer angry or jealous, I was fucking worried.

I should have been marveling at the awesome landscape. Awesome in the true sense of the word. The extraordinary pinnacles of rainbow-colored earth and gullies, all once upon a time under water, rose up majestically in mini mountains, lit in pink and orange hues by the setting sun. I saw some bison in the far distance. All this beauty for nothing. *Where, where, where are you Star?* was all I could think, all I could feel. I missed her and longed for her sassy, smart-ass personality to come sashaying onto our "set", *our* movie. We were partners, she and I. Partners in creation. And I wanted her to be my partner in other ways too.

I pulled out my cellphone and dialed the producer, Pearl Chevalier. There was no fucking way I could film. Not until Star was in front of that lens.

"Hi, Jake," Pearl said, her voice quiet. "I'm so, so sorry about Star. No news from your end, obviously?"

"Not a dicky-bird," I said. "Look there's no way—"

"No, of course not," Pearl cut in, "we'll have

to postpone until she returns. We've got people on it. We'll find her."

"People?"

"Yes, my husband has contacts, you know, people who are used to this sort of stuff."

"Stuff?" My mind was a blank; I couldn't think straight.

"Shady, off the record detective work, you know. They have ways of finding missing people."

"So you don't think Star's done a runner?"

"No. She wanted this part, Jake. Badly. She's a professional, despite her antics. I would never have hired her if I thought otherwise. Her drinking and drugs have never stopped her from being on set before. If that's the case."

I stood there in silence, golden rays of sun warming my closed eyes. I didn't know what to reply.

"We'll find her, Jake, don't worry."

I pressed END to stop the lump in my throat choking into tears.

I had Pearl Chevalier in my mind's eye. A billionaire's wife who could have practically passed for Charlize Theron's double. A woman who had it all: wealth, power, beauty, a happy family, and didn't need this film the way I did. Didn't *need* Star the way I did. She was probably just trying to placate me. Make me feel as if everything would be hunky-dory when I knew we were heading into some sort of nightmare.

Because it had suddenly dawned on me: *Star Davis is a megastar*. What if some bastard had kidnapped her? Then I thought of Leo and I ruled that possibility out. No, he could have passed for one of her bodyguards and was a protective type; he wouldn't have let anyone near her. Nothing made sense.

Nothing made *any* fucking sense.

I LAY HUDDLED in Leo's arms, never having needed a man so much in my entire life. After going to the bathroom, we dozed off together— the drug was doing that to us—knocking us out again soon after we woke up. At least we felt comfort in the rhythm of our breaths, glad not to be in this horror alone. Somehow, I felt safe with Leo, although I knew I wasn't.

I WOKE UP, I don't know how much later, and

the first thing I did was massage the bruise on my neck where the needle had been jabbed in, hoping to God that Travis hadn't injected me with some sort of lethal virus used for chemical warfare, or some crazy shit like that—if it really was Travis—I still couldn't be a hundred percent sure. Had we been kidnapped by some other nut-job? It was a possibility.

Leo sat up, looking less pale than a while earlier. He squinted his eyes. The neon-light was still on.

"You really think your own brother would pull something like this?"

I stretched out my arms above my head. "He hates me, Leo."

"How could anyone hate their own sister? Impossible, no?"

"Jealousy. He feels like his life came to an end when his dad met my mom. He had a complex about being a freckly redhead. He was also asthmatic. I was already acting. He was dyslexic and couldn't learn lines. He tried. My agent took him on but it didn't work out. He couldn't act to save his life. I was the breadwinner. I got good grades in school; he sucked. It was a lot of things."

"Yeah, but . . . you're grown-ups now. Get life."

"Get a life?" I laughed at Leo's accent, always missing pronouns. He was cute when he spoke.

"I'm starving," he said. "Feel like shit. Headache still."

"Me too." I managed to stand and made my way over to the trash can, led by the smell of hummus and pita bread. I picked the take-out bag out of the trash and smelled it. "Fuck him."

"What?"

"He's poured bleach on the food. Yeah, it's Travis alright who's abducted us—just the kind of thing he'd do." A memory came back to me of how he'd pissed on my birthday cake once. *Urinated on my birthday cake!* That's how screwed up he was. I looked around the square room that had obviously once been some sort of office. The bed was empty except for the sheets. Our clothes were nowhere to be seen. Our cell phones gone. Leo's watch: gone. I shuffled over to one of the blacked-out windows, feeling a little exposed in just my bra, panties, and thigh-highs. "There's thick tape all over this. Are you able to get up and help me?"

Leo staggered to his feet, his large, muscled frame swaying, trying to find balance. He gripped his head with his hands. "Feel like someone smashed me on head with baseball bat."

"Well, at least we didn't wake up wrapped in cellophane like mummies, with a knife at our cheek."

"*What?*"

"*Dexter*. You watch that show?"

"Oh yeah, once or twice. I hope your brother isn't serial killer."

"No, just a cereal eater and a crazed psycho."

"Yeah, well, if it is him who's done this to us, he must be pretty fucked up. I need a drink." Leo lurched off to the bathroom, and I heard him frantically drink from the faucet. The drug had dehydrated us both, obviously.

I clawed my nails into the edges of the shiny gray duct tape, picked at it and tried to pull it off. "This is stuck down good," I shouted out.

Leo reappeared, water splashed all over his face and body. "We need a knife."

I tried to laugh. "Naked and knifeless."

We set to work on the duct tape, my nails breaking in the process. Finally, a corner came off, then more, until we managed to peel away the black paper. The window was triple-glazed. "Fuck," said Leo. And then he screamed in anger, "It's fucking un*openable*!"

We looked at each other and then the view below. We were high up, alright. Probably the thirtieth floor. The only skyscrapers in LA were Downtown. And because of earthquakes, they were scarce. I recognized some of the buildings below. "Well, at least we know where we are," I said.

"Fat lot of good, though. We have no way of telling anyone. At least we can turn off that fluorescent light. I still feel like shit. Can't think straight. What now?" He looked up at the ceiling. "You think we can smash through and find air-con ducts—some way to get fuck out of here?"

"We need a ladder. Maybe you're strong enough to smash through. Me? I can hardly stand."

"We can try later. I feel like all my energy has been sucked out," Leo said. "We need to rest up.

Get strong again."

I shrugged. "Nothing to eat. No TV. No books. No way of communicating to anyone, unless we scream till we're blue in the face, but it looks like this room is very well soundproofed. We can take a shower, sleep, and tell each other stories, and hope that my brother appears, so I can find out what the fuck he wants from me and put an end to this."

"Meanwhile we can—" Leo's look was lascivious, his eyes half-mast. Sex. That's what Leo encapsulated: sex. He was no-holds-barred Sex on legs. Even in this sorry state.

"Nice try, Leo."

"You're beautiful, Star. You're naked, except for those skimpy little black panties, stockings, and bra. You think I haven't noticed your delicious body in that sexy getup?"

My lips tilted into a wonky half-smile.

"You're beautiful, Star," he said again. His gaze was intense. I'd say he was undressing me with his eyes but as I was already practically undressed . . .

I thought of Jake, How he'd told me he loved me then swallowed back his words. My eyes flicked down to Leo's chiseled abs and defined chest. He was beautiful too. A raw, dirty beauty— the kind you wouldn't bring home to mother but you fantasized about late at night. The kind you'd secretly like to have ravage every single inch of your body. But not me. I was looking for a *real* relationship. The fairy tale. And until that came along, I wouldn't be giving myself to anybody, least of all a rugged, tattoo-clad Russian, who habitually fucked a whole lot of women, drank copious amounts of vodka, probably gambled, and probably got into fights. Russian/Ukrainian, whatever he was.

"I'd really like to make love to you, Star. Fuck you, too. But make *love* to you—savor your body, taste you, make you come hundred different ways." He cupped his groin—he was hard. Typical. There he was, wiped out by the drug, yet he could still get an erection.

His brashness made me want to laugh but the situation we were in was no laughing matter. "Not now, Leo. Please. We need to figure a way out of here."

"If we're going to die, or get chopped up or

whatever, least we can do is go out with passion in veins."

He certainly had a way with words and I couldn't help smiling. "Wish we had something to eat," I said, changing the subject.

"I can eat your pussy. We can both offer each other plenty nourishment."

I smirked and pushed at his rock-hard chest. "No, Leo."

"Just taste, I'm hungry too."

Boy, was he persistent. I made my way to the door and banged my fists on it with all my might, yelling as loudly as my lungs would muster: "Help! Somebody help us!" But my sounds were muffled—the room swallowing my screams. It seemed hopeless.

Completely and utterly hopeless.

I T WAS six a.m. when the phone rang. Thirty-six hours had passed since they'd been missing. I had personally paid for helicopters to hunt Star down. 24/7 detectives around the clock. I jolted up from the sofa, knowing that the news would be either really good, or disastrous. "Hello?" Finally I'd fallen asleep, all of five minutes ago.

"Sorry to wake you, Jake. Alexandre Chevalier here." The accent was French, the voice deep. For a moment I couldn't fathom who it was. Then I remembered: the man who gave Mark Zuckerberg and Twitter a run for their money—no, a *sprint* for their money—Alexandre Chevalier, CEO of HookedUp, the biggest social media company in history, which had then bought up half of Hollywood. Pearl's young husband. Sinfully powerful and wealthy for a man his age. Any age. A force. People had told me he was a ruthless businessman, but when I met him one time, he was charming.

He went on, "We've been interviewing Star's friends and staff to get some kind of lead," he told me. "Looks promising. Her cell was clean though—stripped of messages, calls—whoever took her knew what they were doing."

I replied groggily, "What have you found out?"

"The cell may have been wiped clean, but we can still extract data," he said. "I just wanted to tell you to sit tight another day or so. Don't wrap up filming yet. Give us a few days more. We'll get there. My niece is on it."

This conversation was getting more surreal by the second. Who *was* this guy? "Your *niece*?"

"Elodie. Between you and me she's good at this sort of stuff: hacking, getting into people's computers and so on. The private investigators you hired seem a little bit slow on the uptake, so we needed to act. Anyway, Jake. Stay put, we'll cover all costs; obviously everyone will be kept on full pay. Let the cast and crew know they can go sightseeing—see the Presidents' heads or whatever. I'll keep you posted." He hung up.

It was a great feeling to know that other people cared too, but if the Chevaliers thought I was going to simply sit around and twiddle my thumbs until they found Star, they had another thing coming. I had to find her—get on the case myself. The image of Star's face was imprinted in my mind: her wide smile, her shining, hypnotic blue eyes, her long blond hair that cascaded around me when she kissed me in places that now made me shudder. Her full, sexy lips. Her innocence and her arrogance, her vulnerability and her cockiness. Her quirky intelligence. I took a deep breath and begged silently to whoever was listening to bring her back to me.

All in one piece.

And then I thought of something: my dog.

Star and Fierce had gotten close. Her clothing

was still at my house. He had an amazing sense of smell—after all, Rhodesian Ridgebacks were originally hunting dogs. I decided to go to Star's house where the Lexus had been dumped in favor of her Porsche.

Perhaps Fierce could pick up her scent.

19
Star

L EO AND I spent hours trying to gain access to the room's false ceiling. He could lift me, but with no tools to help us I could do no more than thump with my fists. And with no ladder or chairs in the room, he couldn't get high enough to exert enough force either.

"What would James Bond do now?" Leo asked.

"He'd have some sort of laser watch that could cut walls in two or some other newfangled gadget."

I padded in my stocking feet—neither of us had shoes—over to the only place we could sit comfortably, and I slumped down on the mattress, exhausted by our efforts. We hadn't eaten for more than what seemed like forty-eight hours and our stomachs were rumbling. We'd taken showers and there was nothing more for us to do than rest up. I lay back, my head propped under my hands. Leo also came to lie on the bed. We didn't exactly have any furniture around here so this bed was it.

"You were in prison?" I asked.

"Yeah, how do you know?"

"What you said about the light blinding you after you got out of your cell. What were you in for?"

"Robbery. Breaking into safe. Also man-slaughter."

I swallowed. Nice, I was hanging out with a murderer. "Who did you kill?"

"My sister's rapist."

"No shit. Jeez. Was she okay?" I heard my words: more concerned with his sister—not caring that he'd actually killed a man. Strangely, I admired him for it.

"No woman is okay after rape. That's what people don't get. Rape isn't something that happens in a moment. Rape is for life. Rape never leaves your soul, your memory. She can never be the person she was before."

Leo was the first person I'd met who'd killed somebody. Somebody who wasn't in the armed forces, anyway. "How did you kill him?"

"Just bare hands. My temper took over, you know?"

"But you didn't serve so long for manslaughter. I mean, you're only twenty-six."

"My uncle arranged for my escape. Why I moved to London."

"I see." I lay there and closed my eyes, trying to imagine everything. If Leo had managed to escape from prison, maybe he could think of a way out now. "How did you get out?"

"My uncle bribed guard. Long story. Not pretty. What about you, Star? You have story about past?"

"I'm just trailer park trash who made good," I said, feeling this to be almost true, although it was so far back in my life history that it didn't seem real.

"Trash? Never. You were born princess."

I sat up and opened my eyes. Leo was gazing at me with genuine admiration. I felt my chest tighten. "Nice tats," I told him, not knowing what else to say.

He laughed. "Don't be sarcastic."

"Actually, they're kind of cool, in a weird sort of way. What do they mean?"

"Hierarchy, disgrace, achievement. Take your pick. In Ukraine tattoos tell story about convict or criminal: date and place of birth, crimes committed, camps or prisons where time is served, even psychological profile."

I moved closer to him. "What does this cat mean?" I asked, running my finger along the curve of his bicep and around his arm, following the pussycat's black, smudgy tail.

"It means I'm thief."

"Is that an achievement or a disgrace?"

"You remember Robin Hood? It was *that* kind of robbery. So both, I guess."

"Why are your tats so . . . "

"Fucked up?" I nodded in agreement. "Tattooing is illegal in jail," Leo explained, "so prisoners make tattoos by melting down boot heels and mixing solution with blood. The guy who did it used a sharpened guitar string attached to motor from old tape recorder. That's why mine look like this. The way you get treated by other prisoners depends on tats you have. Sometimes guys hold you down and force them on you."

"Like what's considered bad?"

"Rat means prisoner who steals from other convicts. Heart inside white triangle—that's sign of child rapist. Not cool, obviously. Those guys get raped by other prisoners all the time."

"Did you get raped?"

"No. I had ways of protecting myself."

"Lucky."

He nodded. "Prison breeds violence. Nobody finds redemption there." He hung his head. His words filled the silence of the room. *I* was now experiencing what he had gone through. Sort of. We were locked up. Unable to escape. But unlike a real prison, we didn't even know why we were here.

I delicately traced my thumb around an image of a lion, and a torn pirate flag, edged with swords, that started on his chest and ended at the last ridged abdomen of his stomach. "And this one?"

"That means I have no-conformist philosophy. Think outside box."

I understood that. A man who had come from a rough, terrifying world, and he'd had the balls and imagination to start afresh in film school—that made him unusual. Jake had been born into movies—it was easy for him. But Leo had had to fight for his dreams.

"You told me you have a sister. Any other siblings?" And I added, with no pause for breath, hungry for information, "What about your parents?"

"Parents are dead. Mom was not good communist. She 'died' in car accident just after I was born. Dad had muscular dystrophy. No joke in my country when you can't pay medical bills. My sister—she's all I have."

"I'm so sorry." The weight of his words stung me to the core. I wished I had been able to speak of my brother with such love, such compassion. "Where is she now?"

"In London. She works as *au pair* to children. She's smart, my sister."

"What's her name?"

"Larissa."

"No kidding? My shrink's called Narissa with an N!"

"You have shrink? Why?"

"It's no big deal. All Americans have shrinks if they can afford it. Well, therapists anyway. Someone gets paid to hear your bullshit sob stories. That way, you don't bore your friends."

Leo laughed. "You could never be boring, Star. Star, is that your real name?"

"No. Diane is my real name. But my agent came up with Star when I was, like, seven, and it stuck. I don't know who Diane is anymore."

"You can't run away from your past though."

"You're right. In my heart and soul I'm still a little girl who grew up in a trailer park. Once you've been poor, no matter how much money you make, the feeling never leaves you."

"Yeah, I had enough watery soup to last lifetime. Enough mugs of tea."

"But you still like your Russian vodka."

He laughed again. "You take the boy out of vodka but not vodka out of boy."

"So going to film school and working on movies was a big change, huh? Being creative?" I tried to sound upbeat. Hearing his story about his dead parents, his jail time, what his sister went through, and the situation we were in now, made me want to burst into tears—I identified with him so much. But tears weren't going to get us anywhere.

People always think that in times of trouble you should act in a certain way. Most folk would have expected me to weep. But when there is no certainty—about anything—your mind protects you. When hit with *real* adversity—something you have no control over—you have to stay calm. That's what I was trying to do: stay calm.

"Film has saved my soul. Saved my life," Leo said quietly.

I thought of Jake. Of how I should be on set right now and it was killing me. How he probably thought I'd let him down. With Leo gone too, I wondered if everyone was suspecting we'd run off together somewhere. I felt a lump in my throat. "So if Jake has done so much for you, giving you such a big chance in the major league, why have you been coming on to me?" I said out of the blue. The words came before I'd had time to think about what I was saying.

Leo shot me a hard look. "Because Jake has girlfriend. Not fair to have cake and eat it too."

His words were like a knife. What Leo said was so true. Jake had a *girlfriend* and if I'd meant anything to him—anything at all, he'd have made sure that Leo kept away from me.

Leo pushed back a lock of hair from my face and traced his thumb along my jawline. "And more to point, I feel bond between us. I saw you in prison uniform and it did something to me. How you acted, Star. It was like you were *me*. Like what I went through. You *knew*. You *know*. How? It wasn't acting, it was real."

A chill shot up my spine and goose bumps spread over my arms and legs. What could I say? That it *was* real to me? That when I act, I feel everything from my head to the tips of my toes? I *am* my character. I transform and feel every breath my character feels, every emotion. Being an actor is no picnic. You live like a schizophrenic—you *are* multiple personalities and it can be painful and confusing.

"Isn't just your beauty, Star. It's deeper. I'm attracted to your soul, your heart, to what's inside of you."

I thought again of how I should be filming, not here in this horrendous predicament. "I'm cold," I said, and I was.

"Come here, baby, let me warm you up."

We lay together, and I nuzzled my nose on Leo's warm chest. He was warm all over—another reason I needed him. He wrapped his arms around my shoulder and covered me with the sheet, while he stroked my hair. The sound of his breathing sent me into a deep sleep.

Travis is holding me down, his hands on my wrists as I'm kicking and screaming at him to let me go.

"Brad, come on, I told you, she's yours, you can fuck my sister—be my guest."

"Let me go, you asshole!" I screech, as close to his ear as I can. I try to kick up my knees into his back, but he slips to one side and I miss.

Brad stands there and chuckles nervously, his hands pushed into the pockets of his long, flowery-print swim shorts. He's smoking a joint. "But she's a virgin, dude, and she doesn't want it."

My leg flies up again. "Let me fucking go, you douchebag!"

"Anyone else? She's for the taking, dudes. My sister needs to lose her virginity, first come, first served."

"I'll do it, Trav, she's hot." It's his half-wit sidekick, Caleb. His tongue is practically hanging out, his big Dumbo ears flapping with excitement, the zits on his forehead glistening like tomatoes on fresh pizza.

I hiss at him, "You come near me, asshole, and I swear I'll pour acid all over your new car."

"Whoa, calm down, vixen bitch!"

"I mean it, guys. Anyone touches me and you're dead meat."

"Little Miss Prissy Cock-Tease!" my brother shouts in my face. "You deserve to be raped because you prick-tease guys and lead them on."

"Let me go, Travis, or I swear I'll run away from home and there'll be no money for any of you! Get it? **No money**! You'll all have to get food stamps because Star Bank Incorporated will be closed!"

He shrieks with laughter. "I don't think so, bitch! Dad's got control until you're eighteen so suck on that, you *whore!"*

"What's going on in here?" It was Dad, standing in the doorway, his voice trembling. "You let go of Diane, right now, young man. And you? Billy, isn't it?"

"Brad, sir."

"You leave this house with your . . . your **drugs,** *immediately. You too, Caleb. And you also, Robby. No more horsing around."*

I look up at my father with gratitude, but he says, "And you, Diane. We're a **family***. We all work so hard to keep you where you are. We are* **all** *responsible for your success. We are a* **team***. I don't ever want to hear threats like that again. We are a* **loving family** *and we look out for each other. Now I want you two siblings to apologize to each other."*

"But, Dad, Travis was trying to—"

"I won't have this nonsense in my household."

All I can think to myself is, **I'm getting the hell out of this dysfunctional nest of vipers the second I can.**

WHEN I WOKE UP, it was pitch dark again. I realized that Leo and I were going to have to mark the time going by, maybe with soap on the bathroom wall, as we had nothing else to do it with. No pen. Zilch. It was the first time I'd been without my cellphone since I could remember. A tinny silence was ringing in my ears. We could hear nothing outside this room, except the odd faint siren going by, or honking of traffic, dim and low in the distance through the triple-glazed windows. All we had was each other and it made me know that I needed Leo. I *needed* him. I had never needed anyone before. Having a mother as an addict and earning all the money for the entire family can make a person pretty self-reliant. But wealth and money meant shit right now. I sat up, Leo still by my side, fast asleep. A strong smell of food caught in my nostrils.

"Leo," I whispered. "So sorry but I'm going to have to turn on the light." I covered his face with the sheet and felt my way to the door. Being so high up meant there were no streetlights to illuminate the room. I couldn't work out where the strong food aroma was coming from. My imagination? Like when people see a mirage of water in the desert?

The overhead florescent light flooded the bare room and, just beside the door with no handle, were several shopping bags of groceries. Ten or so. I leaped upon them like a kid with candy, not understanding how we had missed our one opportunity to attack our visitor and get the hell out of our prison when we'd had the chance. But we still had that drug in our veins, coupled with weakness for not having eaten for so long—no wonder we'd conked out cold.

I grabbed at the groceries. Mostly tins of things—non-perishable items that would last for years. It made me nervous, the amount of food spilling out of the bags; was this to be our new home? And why? What did my brother want from me? Then I looked at the tins. They were the old-fashioned kind that you needed a can-opener for. My heart sank. Another head-game of Travis's.

"What's going on?" Leo groaned—his head buried under a pillow to block out the harsh light.

"Food's arrived. But—"

"How?"

"Someone shoved it all through the door when we were sleeping."

"How the fuck did we miss that?"

"I don't know and it pisses me off. We could have jumped him if we'd been more on the ball." I pulled out a ready-made roast chicken—which must have been what I'd smelled. Everything was either a tin that couldn't be opened, or meat. No can opener. Packets of salami, ham, and turkey.

Tears—tears that I didn't even think I had in me—began to flow out of my stinging eyes. "The bastard." I could feel my body shake.

"Star, what's wrong, baby?"

"I don't eat meat. This is Travis's power game. He wants to break me." I sifted through the bags some more. Meat, meat, and more meat. And . . . a family-size pack of condoms. I knew well what that message meant.

Leo jumped up from the mattress. "I'm sorry, is it really that bad, Star? You're hungry, so eat."

"I can't eat an animal that's been tortured. Suffered in a tiny cage so small it can't turn around, pumped full of antibiotics, with its beak sawn off and . . . " I didn't want to go on. There was nothing worse than a preaching vegan. Each to their own. But I didn't want to be preached to either.

"You don't have to watch me eat, but I'm ravenous," he said. "Give me that chicken, will you? Leo tore his teeth into the cold roast chicken—delicious by his standards, but there wasn't one single morsel for me here that wouldn't make me vomit.

I could hear Travis laughing now—a hilarious joke—all on me, his pathetic little sister.

What a sicko.

I skulked off to the bathroom, not knowing where else to go. After brushing my teeth and washing myself, I shuffled back to the bed, pulled the sheet over my head and conjured up the most beautiful image I could: warm Caribbean water and sugar-white sand. A palm tree making dappled shade—me lying beneath. The sound of gently lapping waves. A huge, juicy watermelon.

I tried to lull myself to sleep.

I FELT THE NOW familiar warmth of Leo's strong body pressed up against me, both of us in the spoon position. He'd turned out the glaring light and we were once again shrouded in darkness. He'd done me the favor of brushing his teeth; I'd heard him for a full fifteen minutes in the bathroom earlier. I could feel his minty breath on my shoulders as he enveloped his muscly arms around my now skinny body, weak with hunger. I was drifting off. I felt whispery kisses on the nape of my neck, as he threaded his fingers through my hair. The rhythm of his breath grew deeper, stronger, and a finger traced down my backbone causing a shiver to run up my spine. My nipples peaked as I sensed the ridge of his rock hard erection press up against me.

"You're so beautiful, Star," he whispered in my ear. "I'm sorry about crude things I said earlier—I was just teasing. Just being dirty boy."

I pretended I didn't hear. But my body couldn't help itself. This dirty boy was turning me on. My bottom eased back against him, comforted by his warmth, his proximity. That was all it took to encourage him. His large hands slid around to my front, slowly clinching my waist and up to my breasts. His touch was unexpectedly soft—not the brute I had imagined at all. He rolled his thumb and finger on my nipple and my eyelids started to flutter with desire. I wanted to stop him but couldn't. I heard myself let out a little moan.

"Oh baby, I know you feel like you're in Hell right now, but I can take you to Heaven, if you'll let me." It was the kind of pick-up line I'd laugh at normally, but coupled with his sensuous touch, it made total sense. Sensuous/sense—my hunger had me almost delirious. I was prone to low sugar levels at the best of times and all I'd had was water. Right now I was in no mood to fight him off.

Leo continued stroking me, his hands traveling south. I felt a finger slip into my panties and rest on my clit. He tapped it lightly. He repeated this several times—the rhythm changing, circling his other hand around my breasts, not touching the nipple. I ached for more, wanting direct contact on my erogenous zones—he knew what he was doing. He was waiting for me to give the okay signal.

"Please," I heard a girl's voice whimper that I hardly recognized as my own. I wanted more. My heart was beating erratically. He slipped his finger a few inches further down.

"So wet, my beautiful Star." His finger eased inside me as his huge erection pressed up against my butt, straining against his boxer briefs. He kissed my neck again, passionate this time, nipping me, as he plunged his fingers in deeper, and he groaned in my ear.

I felt my body turn so that I was facing him, and in the darkness our lips met. My mind was in turmoil—a sort of beautiful chaos—floating, dreaming, transcending earthly reality, but my physical body was giving way. I wanted to control myself, but I just wasn't sure if I could hold out any longer.

I felt like I was falling . . .

The story continues . . .

#3 ***Shining Star*** (the conclusion) OUT NOW!

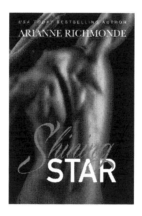

To be the first to hear about future Arianne Richmonde releases sign up to my mailing list. (http://ariannerichmonde.com/email-signup/)

Thank you so much for choosing ***Falling Star*** to be part of your library and I hope you enjoyed reading it as much as I enjoyed writing it. If you loved this book and have a minute please write a quick review. It helps authors so much. I am thrilled that you chose my book to be part of your busy life and hope to be re-invited to your bookshelf with my next release.

If you haven't read my other books I would love you to give them a try. The Pearl Series is a set of five, full-length erotic romance novels. I have also written a suspense novel, *Stolen Grace*.

The Pearl Trilogy
(all three books in one big volume)

Shades of Pearl
Shadows of Pearl
Shimmers of Pearl
Pearl
Belle Pearl

Join me on Facebook
(facebook.com/AuthorArianneRichmonde)

Join me on Twitter
(@A_Richmonde)

For more information about me, visit my website
(www.ariannerichmonde.com).

If you would like to email me:
ariannerichmonde@gmail.com

Made in the USA
Middletown, DE
13 January 2017